D1460147

Issue 16 Autumn 2019

**Award winning science fiction magazine**

**published in Scotland for the whole world to enjoy.**

ISSN 2059-2590

ISBN 978-1-9993331-6-4

Shoreline of Infinity is available in digital and print editions.

Submissions of fiction, art, reviews, poetry, non-fiction are welcomed: visit the website to find out how to submit.

www.shorelineofinfinity.com

Publisher

Shoreline of Infinity Publications / The New Curiosity Shop

Edinburgh

Scotland

011019

Cover: Stephen Pickering

# Contents

**Shoreline of Infinity**
**Science Fiction Magazine**
**Editorial Team**

*Co-founder, Editor-in-Chief & Editor:*
Noel Chidwick

*Co-founder, Art Director:*
Mark Toner

*Deputy Editor & Poetry Editor:*
Russell Jones

*Reviews Editor:*
Samantha Dolan

*Non-fiction Editor:*
Pippa Goldschmidt

*Copy editors:*
Andrew J Wilson, Iain Maloney,
Russell Jones, Pippa Goldschmidt

*Manifold thanks to:* Richard Ridgwell

**First Contact**

www.shorelineofinfinity.com

contact@shorelineofInfinity.com

*Twitter:* @shoreinf

and on Facebook

# Pull up a Log

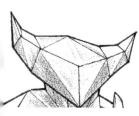

**I thought it was time** we drew* your attention to the works of the artists in Shoreline of Infinity. We have a group of regulars who this issue are represented by Stephen Pickering, Dave Alexander and Jackie Duckworth. Dave is legendary: he's worked on *Commando* and comics such as *Electric Soup*. Dave inspired us in the early days of Shoreline and created our original iconic spacesuited figure staring out into infinity. Stephen's covers make for a splendid display, and you can read more about his plans with the characters on this cover at the inside back page. Jackie is a Cambridge based illustrator and printmaker, and is often visible running her art stall at science fiction conventions all over the UK. Her delightful website is at: www.jackieduckworthart.co.uk

For *Shoreline of Infinity 16* we are debuting two great new artists: Andrew Owens and Emily Simeoni. Andrew and Emily contacted us and after Mark saw their work, he snapped them up. I think you'll agree they are both somewhat special. Off you pop and read the stories but before you dive into the words of wonder, take a moment to enjoy the illustrations.

*no apologies

—*Noel Chidwick, Editor-in-Chief*
*October 2019*

# Mercury Worms

## Petra Kuppers

**A**lex screamed for the earthworms. She screamed for the brown promise of their spring wriggling. Once, when she was about ten years old, she had walked into the forests not far from the house she shared with her grandparents, parents and sister. She could still feel the suck of the earth on her rubber boots, the ever-present grind deep inside her knees, the clammy feel of rotten wood as she tore at the earth. She remembered the plank that had locked like a vacuum seal in the dark moor soil. It came up with a sigh, with a stink, and there were brown earthworms between the ghost-white root fingers. Earth undulated, like a dragon's spine, hidden nostrils behind tree stumps. The path was a muddy snake. Dripping leaves glued to branches like vines in Tarzan movies.

The ghost fingers reached out for years, cool and hot, cauldron breath in her bones. She saw snake cousins in the poor worms, the sideways sway, the desire to crawl back undisturbed into the winter soil. Eventually, the plank lid lay discarded. A tremor had rushed up her legs. And there were more eyes. Simon's eyes. Judgment, dare, and question. Had she been found wanting? That's how it felt, at least now, in sepia-toned view. She longed, she screamed, she reached for the worms.

Alex awoke, the skin of her legs pricking in the regenerator beam. Pink pajamas cloaked electrodes that lay along the smarting bones. Electricity tickled the creaky globes of knee joints. The capsule of her bed pod rested on quakeproof runners, ready to respond to any seismic activity by dropping a large metal frame around her. If that should happen, she would wake up inside a cage, unharmed, with access to communications and emergency food. Her pod was large enough for two, or for a human and a number of companion animals. Alex had chosen to sleep alone, though, and her occasional human bed companions dreamed in their own pods, far away.

Simon had never been among them. A childhood crush hardly ever survived hormones, puberty and adulthood. But strangely, Alex thought to herself as another jolt of regeneration undulated her leg muscles, Simon kept intruding in her thoughts.

The night lay heavy on the desert, and on the newmetal adobe hut that housed Alex's pod. Stars rose and fell, and a moon crept bloody on her spherical path.

In the spaceship far above, cruising past Jupiter, Simon laid hands on the joystick, more a remnant of childhood joys than a necessity. Any real course corrections would be done via control, and there really was hardly any way that a pilot could operate the complex array of systems required to escape planetary velocity.

Psychological tests had decreed that these old forms of control hardware soothed long-distance pilots and their crews. They were memory objects, honoring old forms of being connected to the world through technology.

His fingertips nuzzled the folds of leather covering the semi-spherical object. He remembered caresses: the loving touch of David, Jason, Dwayne. So many others. Names he did not know. Hands that were not hands, but appendages of other kinds. Simon remembered alien drinking holes on distant planets, the queer nod that set up scenes that went far beyond gender, but ended in the same place: shudder, release, an opening. A moment of his childhood rose up again, insistent for days, ever since he had firmly decided to leave. There had been a girl, a different kind of iris opening, and the world had changed.


Alex stirred into the morning. Fake desert air drifted into the pod as she released the locks. She activated the com unit and checked in on her messages. Coffee hummed soon into completion, vitamin capsules, her exoskeleton clicking into place around her midriff, hips, leg bones. She moved over to the old-fashioned table on the patio and started work.

One e-com was intriguing. Alex stared at the picture that had arrived, no subject line, no written or recorded content, but not spam. It was a worm, brown-red, an alien creature in macro-view, round sucking organ mouth open and grasping, sensory hairs around the opening erect and alert.


Simon willed Alex to understand, to ping back, to find a way. He could not think of another ally, only this childhood friend. Each night for weeks now it had come back to him: the moment in the woods, Alex lost to the edge, him afraid, nearly pissing himself, aware of powers circling around the forest glade with its spring melt. There had been Alex, her hands rubbing, legs in wide trembling stance, eyes wide. Beneath her, the tangle of white and brown, moving, escape velocity. The triumph. Release. The image of her wide mouth was burned into him. If only he could reach her now.

The e-com tracked bizarrely, with way-laying stations all over the galaxy. Alex put her best tracker skills to the task, and lost herself as the graphics began their elaborate dance between stars, fields, amplifier ships and relay drones. Then the computer interface blinked and belled.

She had initiated a crawl of the image's data itself, to see if there was any other information encoded in the worm image. Now the image scrolled over her com interface, with little squiggles shadowing the previously smooth picture. There were messages, hairline code tangling into the color commands. The computer had already executed the commands necessary to assemble and translate the binary data. A new message assembled, on top of the straining worm head.

"Please come. Earthworm. Remember the plank."

Alex remembered. The night's dream rose up again, already plowed under in the sequences of everyday life, but now reinstalled in its vivid colors, smell of fecund earth, crisp air, and Simon's stare. He had been initiated. That's what the plank meant here. But what about the worms?

She blinked, and the display shifted back to the tracking software, still tracing the e-com's parabola across known space. Then it stopped. Alex stared at the read-out. Solar system, Explorer-class emigration ship Tiresias, Sender ID: Simon Herflug. Simon from the old forest, on a trajectory far away from poisoned Earth. What did he want from her? She began composing a reply, careful to match the level of security protocols Simon had used – not exactly hard to crack, but requiring specialist tools, enough to escape casual attention. No one was watching too hard.

Simon opened his morning e-coms and bounced on his cot. She had seen it, and replied! With some luck, he could leave knowing that the news was in good hands, and that he could go out with something more like a clear conscience. It might suffice. So he wrote.

*Alex, forgive me for disturbing you, after all these years. I am leaving Earth. It's the final time for me. And on the journey, I recognized what I had been amiss to not lay to rest. The worm and the roots, they are becoming one. I have seen them climb up your legs. I have seen them sink into your limbs. They are moving, now, connecting new orifices in bodies all over old Earth. I don't know if you ever plan to go back to old Earth. But if you do, look for the worm roots. They are still searching for you. I know: they spoke to me, they called me often, and I was afraid to go back. So it's my message to you, a coward's message: you did it then. Can you do it again?*

Stunned. *Simon, what did you do to me?* Alex's hands kneaded, touched the barely responsive flesh of her legs, then the reassuring cool of the wheelchair's titanium. Going back to Earth. Back to the last smells of soil and real water, open water, not the red desert of Mars and its rebreather packs. Would she do it? Was it possible? Of course it was.

Alex had already initiated a credit search, measured against current commonly available transport links back to Earth – a rarely used route direction, but one that was being traversed all the time, by the ships that brought fleeing Earth people to the new pod cities on the planets. She could do it. Credits were fine – it was cheaper than she thought. At least one star glider transport company had their hub not far from her childhood home. Alex had no idea what Simon expected her to do – but she had felt the flower of brown-white tendrils tangle like snakes in her mind, itching to get out.

Alex composed an e-com to the chief of the planetary planning committee, as it was to be her turn to present new hydration plans in group tomorrow. The reports were all done and uploaded. Her physical presence was not an absolute necessity. It rarely was, which was good, given that she often wasn't able to leave her pod at all. She looked at her calendar and dealt with similar smaller issues. All clear. The e-com with the ticket came through just as

she finished a message to her sobriety sister, explaining why she wouldn't be at group, but that she was ok, fine, actually, better than fine for the first time in a long time, with a goal, with a place to go, with a ridiculous but pressing quest. Her side ached, and her toes were frozen like blue ice veins, but she started packing for the 1700 shuttle to the currently deplaning star glider.

Aboard the glider, it was dark and obsidian luster, cushy, but with glints of sharp edges. The authorities had worked out that a journey that evoked womb embrace would lead to a better take-up of new world sensoria upon arrival. Wombs were hardly ever bitingly sharp, of course – but there were also dwindling resources and credit inflation to adjust to.

Wheeling to her belt station on a return journey, rather than an outward journey to the next place, was a weird sensation, and ran counter to all design elements of the glider. Never mind. Alex clicked herself in, initiated the lay flat feature of her chair, and curled as far as the metal frame would permit. Most of the journey would happen in cyro-sleep. She scooped up the tablet lying ready by her console and adjusted the monitoring cap on her head. Within minutes, she was gone, and didn't even notice when the back end of the glider closed, shutting out the last remnant of red Mars light. They took off.

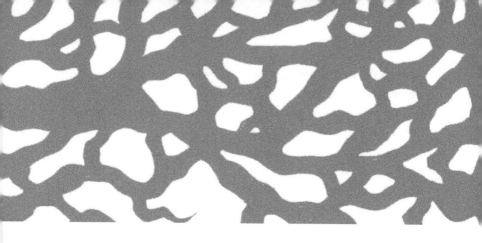

Earth light. To Alex, it just felt like the next morning. She was stiff, needed to both piss and drink copious amounts within seconds of waking. She pissed in her chair pod, knowing that the cleansing routine would take care of it. She had no time to get her wheelchair upright and into the bathroom. The electrolyte-balanced drink helped clear her. At the far end of the glider, the ramp had descended, and morning dawn light broke across the metal. No one was around. The crew might still be asleep, apart from the lonely pilot in their capsule. It was a full Earth day before the glider needed to be got ready for the return journey, full with weather emigrants. So Alex collected her stuff, initiated a quick cleanse, and, still dripping, rolled down.

The light broadened, opened. Her childhood light, her dream light, lumens that were unmatched on exo-planets. She started to cry as the light touched her, air touched her, fabric whistling in the wind. There was a copper tang to the air. Something was off, though – as if a hurricane was coming, a light red-shift, barely noticeable.

Alex rolled across the tarmac, through the station, and out the other end toward ground transport. The tenth self-driving taxi was accessible, so she waited patiently till it was her turn. She gave the address. This was the nearest street address she could remember. The small forest itself had no address, no coordinates that she could conjure up. Alex felt silly, impulsive, gliding noiselessly over half-drowned villages, encroachments of salt-laden seas far into the plains of middle Europe. She felt reasonably confident that her childhood village was still on maps, otherwise the sat nav would have informed her otherwise. About 60 feet above the water-logged strata of old Germany and old Netherland, her taxi flew at medium speed. ETA 24 minutes. Alex stretched, and gazed out at the level horizon.

Eventually, the taxi glided to a halt, opened. The red laser light played across her fingertips as she paid up, then left. She was on solid land, on a road. Around her, houses stood alert and awake, even though it wasn't yet 7am local time. Windows blazed over soggy front gardens, lawns long replaced by rain gardens or sandscapes. To her left, Alex saw the dark fringe of the old forest. It was still there. She wheeled forward.

"Alex. I knew you'd come back."

Alex stopped, wheeled about. She stared. "Foerster." She needn't say more, the tone full of repulse as well as nostalgia. Forester, gatekeeper, old man, leech.

"I know, I know. Water under the bridge, Alex. Sorry for the old days. I got a bit slower."

Alex remembered. It had been normal then, the casual violence, sexual harassment, locker-room talk. Those days were gone, and Foerster must have gone through re-education, given that he was still around and walking freely. She looked for the bulge of an electronic collar around his ankles, found no sign. He stood firm, a walking stick by his side.

"Hey. How is the neighborhood?"

"The same. More and more are leaving. The sun hasn't really been out for 12 years now. Waterlogged. Berlin and Bonn are no help, nor is Strasbourg. It's gone to hell. Where do you live now?"

Alex talked briefly about Mars. They described the land changes they'd lived through: a red sun-up on desert land. The shimmering line of a horizon that is water in water. Heat. Drizzle. Decay, in their different forms. They enjoyed the exchange, an old anchor. Long old stories not exactly forgotten, but laid aside for the sake of finding a spindle, a single sharp moment in the past with which to spear the present.

"How did you know I'd come back?"

"Didn't Simon tell you? The worms are calling for you. Can't you hear them? They are calling you now. We, the old ones, are no good to them."

Foerster stood silent. Alex stared. The edges of the man began to swim, to shift. Was he really there? The light crept up, still not really sunlight, oyster color, luminous grey. It shone through the old man. A breath. He was gone.


Alex's fingers were icy on the wheelchair controllers. She wheeled away toward the forest's dark edges, and their black watercolor light.

It was near noon when she arrived. The forest was thinner and smaller than she remembered. She had to navigate multiple pools and small streams, find ways to measure for depth to ensure that her wheels wouldn't wet to the electronic hubs. So it took a while, even with the rugged all-terrain wheel set. She nearly got stuck on the path's grave-dark soil. The frangible stuff first clung lightly, then packed and caked to everything.

Eventually she found what she thought was the old plank: a rectangular ghost of matter, fungoid silver.

She could hear them now. There was singing here. There was movement, shifting, delay and echo. She wedged one nerveless foot under the edge of what was left, and heaved with her arms and upper back.

The worm was a river in the earth. Its back looked like what she imagined an alligator's skin would look like up close: dikes and canals, patches, all glowing orange and white in the wet afternoon light. Its girth was larger than her waist. It moved, gently, as it pulsed earth through its innards, winnowing and conditioning. The hint of translucency brought her an image of a dark vein of soil.

The worm didn't seem to notice her. It was alive, despite the earth's poison. Her titanium wheels felt clumsy next to the articulating segments of its broad length. She contemplated touching it, but decided against it, didn't wish to become aware of its temperature, the cold-blooded lack of differential. This had never been her, even as the worm's ancestors, or maybe sisters, had found their way in. The worm was transforming the metal poisons, Alex knew in her bones.

What was she to do here? What did this massive worm want from her – guarding a golden, lead, or mercury hoard deep by the river's bottom? Was it inviting her to dance in attendance in dark wells? All very unlikely, laughable, no good to a drowning world.

Alex was cold. But she wasn't giving up. Simon might have been a dreamer, but he was no fool. She couldn't think about Foerster. So she investigated around the worm's pulsing presence. Soon, she found a second weaving, another source of movement, less strong, less grand. It had escaped her, at first, in the giant swelling worm dance. At the edges of the worm's embedment in the earth, white-brown roots formed their own rhythm, a dance that was half complex weft, and half actual movement, an ultra-slow breathing, plant triple-time.

This was her interlocutor, the plant worm that had called, not the ancient giant sucker. Alex stemmed herself up from her chair and then lowered herself down to the soil. The sucking pipeline didn't shift rhythm or otherwise indicate interest. The root worms, though, they knew. They hove up. One rootlet at a time. A worm's sensory organ's grasp upward. A dance in the pattern of a mimosa's leaf uncurling. It came. They came. Alex lay, arranged her legs next to the gap in the earth, her torso outstretched so her face was near the root strands.

She welcomed them. Opening. Mouth open, zippers undone. Cool. Moisture. A squelch as she shifted into a more comfortable position. Around her, skin breathed. Her own skin shifted spectral color, darker, lighter, violet spectrum, brown, purple. Mushrooms drifted spores, spores so long extinct in so many sites of Old Earth. The waiting rootworms had held on to these tiny black dots, and unclasped the spores from thin mantles wrapped around their writhing lengths. The spores entered Alex, in multiple sites, and her eyes color-shifted, too, a deep blue shining upward.

The giant worm next to her in the earth felt it, shifted infinitesimally. It unleashed new young ones, new root graspers that melded with and opened Alex. Code flowed. Nerve and metal knitted, blood and plasma. New sensations climbed up from blue toes. The back of knees signaled in. The back of a mountain range answered. The moon sent Morse-codes full of gravitational pulls. Alex's liver felt them, and responded, giving up its meld-information, beeping back secrets to plant mitochondria. She noted ice under her soles, individual crystals first burrowing toward, then breaking into her flesh. They rocked themselves into her, she into them. She breathed with them.

Slow, equalizing, ice and heat and rain and the slow tilt of a sun's axis. They laid there, entwined, till the sun broke through above Alex, the worm, the nest of weaving tendrils, creatures, rootworms. The sun warmed her, offered a new surface against which to assemble. Eventually, seeds safely deposited, the rootlets withdrew from orifices they had so tenderly explored.

Alex sat up, hand reaching for her wheelchair. The metal had warmed under the late afternoon sun, an orange-red ball so long unseen in these latitudes. She used a combination of strong hands and numb feet to find enough leverage to pull the plank back over the forest worm bed. The sun might do damage, withdraw too much water. This was better.

Alex shifted back in her seat, turned her chariot, and wheeled downward, her nose open to the mold smell of fertile soils and decaying leaves. What had been unraveled was knitting together again. The sun kissed her face, and a mercury tear ran down her cheek.

**Petra Kuppers** is a disability culture activist and a community performance artist. She is author of the poetry collection *PearlStitch* (2016) and the queer/crip speculative short story collection *Ice Bar* (2018). She lives in Ypsilanti, Michigan, where she co-creates Turtle Disco, a community arts space. She teaches at the University of Michigan.

# You and Whose Army

## Allen Ashley

**W**e **had become accustomed** to the regular requirement of warding off Rawlinson's paper army. These magically ambulant soldiers were either controlled remotely by Rawlinson himself or else worked on a gestalt principle. Which meant that unless we disabled or destroyed at least forty or fifty per cent of them during the initial stages of the battle, they would keep on coming. Amassing. Amalgamating.

Generally, being paper, they carried no weapons. Their technique was to isolate one of our number and overwhelm him or her, smothering our hapless colleague in a perverted kiss of life that would render our friend incapable, inoperative... dead. I had almost suffered that fate on two occasions and even now I woke up during the night battling against my sleeping bag and its claustrophobic constrictions.

Such brushes with death leave one both battle-hardened and psychologically scarred. Sometimes I feel that my soul holds a huge yawning void that almost yearns for the touch and the crush and the overload of paper to fill it with purpose, to counteract the emptiness.

We fight to preserve what remains of our way of life and during the longueurs I have sometimes worried that our cause is meaningless, empty...

"Stop staring into the void of the future, Paul," my colleague Shireen tells me. "It's an unknown country. Live in the moment."

I want to protest that I am keeping a lookout for the next sortie by Rawlinson's mob, but she can see that I am facing in the wrong direction.

"Maybe at least the next five minutes," I smile. "Fail to prepare; prepare to fail."

She rolls her tired brown eyes then goes off to see whether HQ have sent further supplies to us soldiers out here on the crisp front line. And who can blame her for terminating a conversation that has been reduced to aphorisms and chiasmus?

We have knives – often long-bladed and curved like something out of *Arabian Nights*. On quiet afternoons we flex our biceps and forearms, practising parabolas that will slice through our enemy. It takes two of us to deploy scissors – one to hold the victim and one to cut. Guns have proved ineffective, especially as our opponents have lately developed a smoother, shinier surface which tends to deflect or even bounce back towards us our close-range artillery shots. We have lost more of our number to stray bullets than we have inflicted casualties upon their force with gunfire.

Shireen returns with cups of lukewarm coffee and a couple of thin and chewy protein bars. These make me reflect that normal life must be going on somewhere, people are working in fields or factories and offices. That's one familiar drudgery we are seeking to preserve even though it seems a million miles and a thousand years away from the here and now.

We tried water cannon. The cubic volume required to render Rawlinson's paper puppets drenched and inoperative was immense and unsustainable in the long term. But it was a wild, squelchy ride. Had our opponents been fleshy creatures, we would have been swimming in blood at the end of the day. Instead, we waded bravely through their soggy remains with our uniforms water-logged and clinging to our bodies in damp tatters like a skewed reflection of our victims. We celebrated wildly at our eventual watery victory. Shireen's nipples taut and pert against the damp fabric of her shirt called to my hands and mouth like the comforting breasts of a goddess. My own slippery hands were unable to pull down my trousers over the bulge of my post-battle erection but Shireen gladly obliged.

It was a hedonistic night for the whole platoon. Nothing of the sort has passed between Shireen and me since. Top brass decided to turn a blind eye so long as we were all fit for duty the next time it was required of us. I was glad of replacement fatigues when they became available.

"Don't forget weapons check in ten minutes, Paul," Shireen says around a mouthful of biscuit.

"What will have changed since yesterday?"

"Nothing, hopefully. Just keeping us sharp, I guess."

I tip away the dregs of my drink. "The army runs on routine."

"The world runs on routine, Paul. The Earth keeps orbiting the Sun forever, I suppose."

"Quite the philosopher today, Shir."

"Too much time to think. Bring on the action."


Brave words and foolish. Rassy, today's scout, shouts the one word, "Approach!" and we are pinned again.

Just a small detachment this time. And not human.

"Animals. Watch those jaws, Paul."

Like paper teeth would pierce my skin. And yet… and yet I remembered back to a work experience placement when I was much younger and the world was simpler. Tasked with hand-delivering internal mail and a mountain of photocopying duties, I had suffered a succession of paper cuts that had taken weeks to clear up.

The enemies present as huge beasts: ursine, equine and, poetically, a big lumbering tiger moving somewhat unsteadily, mostly on its hind legs. Intimidating, yes. But slow and lacking the agility that defines hand-to-hand combat. Shireen and I work as a close-knit team and soon reduce our enemies to shredded ribbons.

The weather is dry but not warm. Yet we are sweating buckets. And, amid the perspiration, some nervous tears.

She leans into my chest for a brief, brotherly hug – which means she won't discern how wet my face is.

"I don't know how long I can keep up the fight, Paul."

"We'll keep going until it ends."

"Or until it ends us."

Colleagues relieve our duties for the evening and night watches. Tomorrow is projected to be bright and cloudless. I expect a further, more concerted attack. Rawlinson will want to take advantage of the glare and confusion conjured by the combination of sunlight and his ambulant white minions.


Fighting with fire had long been my preferred option and we had been given access to flame throwers some two weeks ago during a spell when we had been losing significant ground on a daily basis. I had wielded my giant torch with boyish abandon, taking down many of the attackers more by luck than skill. Coils of acrid smoke and curls of grey, ashy paper lifted by the breeze marked my successful shooting.

There are strong religious beliefs back home that all life is sacred. I never wanted to kill anyone or anything but… needs must, the battle is always us against them.

Training in the new weapons had been cursory, almost non-existent. As much as we reduced Rawlinson's vanguard to charred ruins that day, we also suffered sizeable casualties within our own ranks. The wounds caused by burning are far less comfortable to witness and to attempt to deal with than the smothering, strangulation and severe bruising that generally characterised our losses. And the smell. Charred hair and skin – I wouldn't be touching any cooked meat for some time.

Our losses due to what was undoubtedly deemed as a most extreme exemplification of "friendly fire" led our superiors to withdraw the new, potent weaponry until we could all be properly drilled. Like we were likely to have a pause in hostilities long enough for that…

I continue to suspect that the real reason is cost-cutting. We are at the front line fighting for our very culture's continued survival yet we are making do with tattered uniforms, second-hand ordnance and paltry equipment. Perhaps they – our unelected and secretive leaders – aren't that invested in our potential victory. Maybe they have contingency plans that would quite happily absorb stalemate or even defeat.

I try to bury the doubt or burn it away with the strength of my conscientiousness. We will fight on regardless.

They are coming en masse.

The sun has barely risen and our eyes are still sanded with sleep but there is no mistaking the sight that approaches from the close horizon. Shireen seems torn between a wry smile and a slow, disbelieving shake of the head. I push back near-death memories from an earlier escapade. Such claustrophobic recollection will do me no good now. Focus on the moment, the current fight –

And we engage. And I'm swiping with knives and slashing with blades and working in teams with giant silver scissors. But we are making no headway. The paper soldiers march onward and threaten to overwhelm us.

I see Dawood struggling against a batch of them. I try to elbow my way across to assist but the enemy is lined up in deep rows that feel impenetrable.

Shireen goes down under their onslaught and this time I do find the energy to spring to her assistance. I haul several of these thin golems off her body and help her back onto her feet.

"Paul," she pants, "Paul, they won't cut. It's…"

I am aware that my actions and those of my platoon seem to be having zero effect.

"It's like… they've got some sort of resin that's hardened up the paper."

"Let's try together," I mutter, and we wield the giant scissors like we have done so many times before. Feeling resistance. Completing that first snip but unable to follow through.

War is always about technology. Necessity for victory drives ingenuity and invention.

But we will not be beaten.

"Throw down your weapons!" I shout above the tumult. "Do as I do." Then, quieter, to Shireen, "Grab him by the shoulder. Now pull. And fold again across the stomach."

Battle-weary, battle-hardened, hungry and bedraggled we may be but still our discipline is strong. In my peripheral vision, I catch my colleagues copying our actions. Soon each of us has two or three of the enemy combatants folded into five or six unequal pieces and prone beneath our booted feet.

There are more still to fight. Thankfully, our technique seems to have confused them and they are milling rather than overwhelming.

"I can't keep my foot on this one forever," Shireen says.

I scrape my captives towards her. "Sit on them," I instruct. "You can probably keep five or six of the folded fuckers still and quiet while we deal with the rest."

Even in the midst of victory, I am thinking: how long can it last? What if reinforcements never arrive to relieve us of our jailer duty?

The last of Rawlinson's paper men have retreated. In what was clearly supposed to be their finest hour, we have found a way to arrest their hideous progress.

Our bent captives are unmoving beneath our equally still bodies.

"What now?" someone asks.

"I remember how to make a perfect edge when you don't have a knife or a ruler," Shireen states.

"Go on."

"Well, you fold down one way then you fold the paper back on itself the other way. You keep doing this until you have a perfect edge or a deep groove. Then you let rip."

I take a look at the seated company around me. If we handle this carefully and methodically, then maybe...

"Great idea, Shireen. Folks, it's going to be a long, hard day. But we need to start to take care of these paper machines until a relief detachment arrives. So, Shireen, if you just gently raise yourself up a few inches, we'll start there. Let's shred these bastards."

Cheers and brief high-fives. Victory. For now.

**Allen Ashley** works as a creative writing tutor with five groups running in north London, including the advanced science fiction and fantasy group Clockhouse London Writers. Allen's most recent book is as co-editor (with Sarah Doyle) of *Humanagerie* (Eibonvale Press, UK, 2018) – an anthology of human-animal liminality stories and poems.

There once was a laddie from Saturn
Who had a bit of a heartburn
Stop eating those rings
They are terrible things
Said his friend, the Duchess of Melbourne.
—*Lilly Hunter*

# The Polite Thing to Do

## Helen French

"We need your assistance," the message began. "Our ship can't fly. We are missing vital elements. You must help us. Best hopes, The Gernigan."

Emily Bottomley was 78 and lived alone in a farmhouse in the middle of acres of land that were no longer tended. Visitors and callers were rare.

She squinted at the screen on her knees – most commonly used as a tray for her dinner plates these days – and read the email again.

It was only polite to reply, wasn't it? Even if at her age she wasn't much good to anyone (thank you, son).

She typed: "Dear Sir/Madam(s), I'm terribly sorry but I don't think I can help you directly. Where are you? Would you like me to call the emergency services? Best wishes, Emily."

She put the lap-screen down and shuffled off to the kitchen, where the air was warm and moist. Emily opened the window over the sink, opened the back door to let a tabby cat in, and started the kettle.

"I have boiled!" it yelled at her a few moments later.

"Yes, dear," she replied, though its listening apparatus had broken long ago. She reached up to the crockery shelf and picked out two mugs. It was an old habit (God bless and miss you, Daniel), that she'd made into a useful one. One for now, one for later. Why reach twice when once will do?

By the time the tea had brewed, the cat had been fed, and Emily got back to the living room, her lap-screen was flashing an angry shade of orange.

She expected a berating note from Oliver: "What am I supposed to think, mother, if you won't answer my calls?"

Instead, it read: "Gernigan cannot tell you where we are. Still locating co-ordinates of our position to rest of world. We are close to you but far from services. But this is emergency. We require morels for engine lift-off. You are only soul in range with morels. Will you help us?"

Emily considered the request. The Gernigan, whoever they were, hadn't offered money, like so many of the pleas that Oliver was always warning her about. Their email address was written in symbols. The English not quite right, but not that wrong. It didn't give much away and yet once again Emily felt inclined to reply.

"Morals? There aren't any here to spare. Those I have are rather stuck with me, I'm afraid."

She sat back once the message had sent and shortly afterwards a loud buzz like a giant bee might make filled the room. The house shook.

Emily held on tight to the side of her armchair, knuckles white with tension.

Daniel would've hated this, she thought. The house he'd built, shaken to its foundations. "What's wrong with a delivery man?" he would've asked.

Eventually the shaking stopped. The buzzing slowly faded, lifting away. Emily pulled herself up and out of the chair with a huff, and went around to the back door.

One sad cracked egg was spilling its guts out onto the ground, yellow trails torn apart by the grass around it. Behind it, brown paper sacks slumped where they lay. The food drone had dropped the bags from the wrong height again.

It took the best part of an hour to get it all in the house and stashed away tidily. Emily's back hurt from craning over, and her arms ached from lifting.

Ordinarily she'd slip off for an afternoon nap at this time, sleep being an easy way to while away the years that she could no longer be bothered with. Today did not feel like an 'ordinarily' sort of day. She checked the lap-screen one more time.

A new email had appeared. "You mistake us! It is morels not morals we require. Take careful note of the letters we use. They are spongy and ridged, pale of base, with a brown crown."

Morels? Emily didn't know what they were talking about. Then the name tickled something at the back of her mind. Mushrooms? She laughed out loud. Yes, they were a type of mushroom! But why should she care?

"I'm sorry dear, but I don't have any mushrooms or morels or whatever you want to call them."

A reply landed within a minute. "But our ship won't fly without them. They are a key part of our fuel-load. We are trapped. We will die."

Surely nonsense?

"What sort of ship?" she fired back. Were they children making mischief?

"Exploratory," they replied. "We are The Gernigan."

Aliens? There had been rumours. Even on the ring-thing, people chattered, said the Senary Council were talking to other beings. Could it be true? She'd tried asking Oliver about it once and

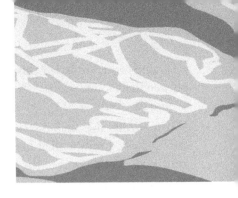

he'd starting asking her about dementia symptoms, so she'd put it out of mind.

They continued. "We are stuck by the glade. Our detector calculates that the nearest significant distribution of morels is in the woods on the other side of your homestead. We ask that you pick some for us, for we can't survive in your atmosphere. The databases we have access to suggest they are best found by bluebells and ash trees and little purple flowers. They are the closest thing your world has to our main crop. Without them we will die."

Emily knew too well what it was like to feel trapped, suffocated. Who would want to face their final days like that?

Why not help them?

There was only one problem: Daniel.

They'd gained permission many years before to have their burial plot in the grounds of their farm, so they could be side-by-side forever in the place that had brought them so much joy.

Then he'd had the gall to die first.

Now she couldn't walk out that way. Oh yes, Emily had buried him there – it was what he wanted, and one day she would inevitably join him. But she saw little point in visiting the place where her wonderful husband was turning to dust, out by the woods. In fact she rarely left home at all.

The lap-screen flashed twice. Two messages.

One was from Oliver. "Mother, I'm going to call this afternoon at 4pm. If you do not answer, you'll leave me no choice but to…"

She clicked onto the second, a single word from the Gernigan, "Please."

Emily dug around in the hallway for her decent walking boots, which were stiff as board but still

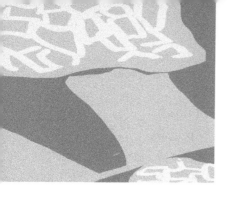

useable. Next came a light jacket; it could get cool in the woods.

She plodded to the kitchen and filled a small bottle of water, which went into one pocket, and then picked up a canvas bag, which she folded up and put into the other pocket. Finally, she put a wrist-screen on for 'just in case'.

The front door opened outwards with a creak. Beyond it, a narrow path led in two directions – stretching to a farm road that would take her to the old sheep fields and to the town ten miles away, or to the valley with Daniel's grave and beyond that, finally, the forest.

I should at least try, Emily decided. I can but try.

All the same, she was surprised by the tremble in her step as she cautiously traipsed down the garden path, at the way her chest shook with each breath.

She followed the grooves in the road left by tractors years ago, worn deep through perseverance. She headed south and it sloped downwards, to a small clearing.

The ground here was rough and wild, heather and flowers and weeds (or were they all weeds if left untended? all wildflowers?) battling for dominance where once grass was cut and children played. Holes were scattered across the way: homes for rabbits, traps for the unsuspecting. The edge of a river was visible in the distance, birds circling above it in the wide blue sky.

It didn't take long to find the mound at the edge of the clearing marked with a simple wooden cross. Emily's breath caught in her throat. Daniel… it had been so long.

It hurt to look at. Emily averted her gaze, looking anywhere save that solemn spot. Her heart beat hard, and then her knees gave in.

She thudded to the ground, damp grass wetting her jeans; it would stain the denim. Her bones ached.

Nothing broken, she thought. Only Daniel.

It was a long while before she stood up again.

Emily walked forward, stopping at the wooden cross. She pressed her fingers to her lips, then down to the cross, worn smooth with age.

"I've nearly forgiven you for leaving," she said.

It was time to head to the forest.

✳

The 'forest' was what the family called it, but it was more like a minor scattering of trees over a couple of acres of land. Enough to hide in as a child, enough to think in as an adult.

Emily saw the bluebells first, a river of petals winding in between tall brown-grey tree trunks that were probably ash.

But where were the mushrooms? She tried digging through the soil at the base of one of the trees. Nothing.

It all felt faintly silly. Sent by aliens to dig up mushrooms? Come off it.

She was exhausted too, and frustrated that she felt that way. This was not what she'd dreamt of for her old age.

Then she spotted a glimpse of purple a few metres away. She'd forgotten about the other sign, the little flowers they'd mentioned. Yet here they were, bravely sticking their heads above the undergrowth.

And what was that? It looked more sponge than plant, but Emily looked closer and yes, it was a mushroom, only not one she'd ever seen before. Her eyes widened. There were fifty or so under these trees. She whistled, loud and clear.

Were they morels? She consulted the checklist. Spongy and ridged – a honeycomb sort of pattern. Pale at the base, brownish at the top. They would do.

Emily packed as many as she could fit into her canvas bag and as soon as she stood up the wrist-screen beeped.

"Our monitors show morels have been moved from their original positions. We assume you have been victorious," the message read. "Find the water by the wooden-cross-field and come to its edge."

Giving herself no time to doubt, Emily retraced her steps, back to Daniel, and back to the cross. The sun was beginning to lower itself down through the sky.

She strode to the river, feeling lighter now her task was done.

And then the water sucked her in.

It was like being pulled down a vacuum, or slipping down a slide at the water-park. The water didn't touch her. She was transported down, down, down into blue-green water, then darkness, protected by some sort of invisible shield.

Then she was on solid ground, only not ground, something like a spongy metal instead, no longer being towed, no longer in water, yet somehow at the bottom of the river. In a ship? Doors closed behind her. A different set opened in front of her. There was no time to panic, only to forge ahead.

Emily tried to stand upright, but the ceiling was too low. She hunched over and followed the passageway, which did nothing for her back, but there appeared to be no alternative.

The air was gloomy and dark, the corridors knobbly and green. It smelt of tea and tobacco and flowers decaying. She seemed able to breathe perfectly well though, which was handy given the circumstances.

It felt like being in a dream, so Emily treated it like one. She started to relax, sure no harm could befall her there. It was too far removed from her life to be real.

She came to a room shaped like an amphitheatre, only the steps seemed to be computers, all flashing lights and winking icons that she didn't understand. Working them were plate-sized yellow-and-brown mottled creatures, something between a flatfish and a giant frog, each one placing flabby limbs onto screens and buttons.

The nearest creature tilted its face upwards at her; its eyes were wise and intelligent. They had to be the Gernigan.

Emily was intrigued rather than scared. She smiled and put the bag of morels down. "I brought them for you," she said, and three Gernigan from further back in the room slithered forward to carry it away.

She knelt down and held out a hand. It felt like the polite thing to do. The creature slid onto her palm, then somehow connected into her mind. First a jolt, and then a presence.

"Welcome and thank you, Emily Bottomley," it thought at her. "These morels were much needed."

"You said you couldn't get them yourselves?" she asked, finding she could very simply think right back at them, and in her dream-like fog she accepted that.

"We are different, you and I," it thought, "but only a little. Your air is missing one element we require, while ours has everything that you need. That's why we could not travel outside of this ship, but you can breathe now. You'd be able to breathe on our homeworld, if your human body could survive the flight to get there."

"It wouldn't?"

"No. But you are welcome to travel with us anyway. Look." It poured images into her brain, showing off their way of living.

The Gernigan had spaceships and technology beyond anything on Earth. Extensive colonies, friendships that lasted a thousand years, mates bonded to one another for life, a whole, full life. It looked wonderful.

"Come," it thought at the end.

"I can't. Can I?" They'd already said she wouldn't get through the journey.

It showed her more. "We can take your consciousness and imprint it onto a new brain in one of our bodies. Spares have been constructed. We carry them, always."

She saw it – a line of the strange creatures somewhere deep in the vessel, waiting to be filled with a soul – she even believed it, began to sense the truth of it. "But what would happen to me? This me, I mean?"

"A faint version of yourself, a copy, would be left inside. Enough to get your form home, but little else. It is of no matter. You would be with us. We would be your family. You saved us."

And they could save her from the bleak doldrums, from Oliver's lectures, from the fear of the outside. A chance for something new. No more sitting at home, waiting for it all to be over...

In any case, it seemed rude to flat out refuse when they'd been so welcoming.

"Will it hurt?" she asked, and that was the last thing Emily Bottomley remembered as a human.

"Mother? Mother!" Oliver yelled, first confused, then angry, as he opened the door of the farmhouse. He'd spent a fortune on the super-shuttle to get there. "Why didn't you answer me?"

When Oliver found her at last, she was asleep on the sofa, mouth open, drooling a little.

He shook her gently by the shoulders. "Mother, wake up. I was worried." She opened her eyes slowly and smiled at him. "Mother?" he asked.

But she couldn't reply.

She heard him, but did not hear him. Was there, but no longer there. The real Emily was flying through the universe, laughing and slithering and celebrating, more alive than she'd been for the longest of times, at last unburdened and free.

Helen French is a writer, book hoarder, TV-soaker-upper, digital project executive and biased parent who grew up in Merseyside and now lives in Hertfordshire, UK. Her short fiction has appeared in Daily Science Fiction and Flash Fiction Online. You can find her on Twitter at @helenfrench.

Toner '19

# The adaptation point

## Kate Macdonald

**F**ourteen children were born on the voyage to Eder 4, but only Vlar survived the first year. Two died before landing, and eleven more succumbed at a rate that left the adults desolate. Respiratory failure during the sandstorms, inexplicable cardiac arrests at night, blood cancers that flourished out of control in weeks, and simple dysentery and exhaustion. The water plague in Year Five killed adults as well. No child thrived except Vlar. The Specialists began to pay the Eder 4 Settlement some attention.

Vlar's survival turned her into a medical specimen. Once Specialists were able to land, her microbial activity was studied exhaustively. All her biota were sampled and her knowledge of clinical procedures became expert. Her immunities were nurtured with clinical attention. Because she was rarely allowed to risk her precious data-ridden body in the field, she was kept with the younger, Settlement-born children. Her maths scores rocketed as her only compensation, and she played pilot games among the tumbling bodies of her three small satellites. But she was tired of babysitting all the time, and pounced on the slightest hint that any of the younger ones would one day be able to play maths games with her.

When she attained eleven years of successful microbial activity she rebelled, heading out one night with a stolen snaptent and a ration sack. Nav had told her about a safe place to camp in the hollows. There had been a vicious but short sandstorm two days before her return, but she'd dug over Field 3 and her tent had not been shredded. She came back after the relay shuttle had left, because she had seen the Specialists go with it.

"The fields are dangerous on your own. What would you have done if a moler smelled you?" said her mother Vanot, irritable but resigned.

"They never touch me. And Nav knew where I was,' Vlar kept her voice confident, but her eyes were on her fingers, checking for biters among the tent's yellow folds.

"Yes, we knew too. But I don't agree that molers wouldn't hurt you. Remember Kav's leg?"

Vlar did remember how long it took Kavit to die from the bite. Dreadful minutes of screaming from pain, then sudden, catastrophic blood poisoning and organ failure within the hour. But she *knew* the molers wouldn't touch her. They'd crept past her open tent door at twilight and dawn without bothering to turn their heads. The biters were the same: they noticed her, but she was not food, or a threat. Vlar wondered how long this would last.

"You could have waited two more weeks.' Vanot still sounded aggravated.

"Why?'

"With the Specialists out of the way, Myennit was going to take you to help check on Site Two. Backup has finished the lifeforms survey, and needs to dismantle. You'd have had a chance at field travel for a change, we know you hate being stuck here. She had to take Nirt instead, and we need him here."

Then Vanot slapped the tent back onto the table. "It'll do. Pack it away." Vlar folded silently, feeling dejected. Vanot turned to look out of the salt-smeared porch window towards the sea. "We're down to three adults now, with the Specialists gone. Bad timing, Vlar. Without Nirt I have to take Borromit to the fields. His eyes are still bad. I should have sent him back to the relay ship for proper treatment.'

"They wouldn't have taken him. They don't take any of us.'

Vanot wasn't listening. "It's all happened at once. The Specialists didn't need to leave when they did; they had months of mission left. The wrong people are in the wrong places at the busiest time. Boll harvest has to be done this week or the molers will take everything, and then Myennit decides she has to set off now to sort out Site Two." Vanot thumped the curving wallframe with frustration. The porch trembled. "I don't know how we're going to do it.'

"I could fly the sled, or Hannit could –" Vlar began.

"No, he can't." Vanot said in the way that stopped argument. "He's stable indoors, and most productive in the greenhouse. I'll take Borromit to the fields, and I want you to get some greens in tomorrow. We need to build up stores again before summer ends, now those Specialists have gone.'

Vlar was back in the nursery again.

The pink and grey lava sand made the walk from the beach a long, slow pull up the dune to the doors of the ship, perched on its solid basalt outcrop. The children pulled the hovering landsleds packed with sand greens behind them. They brushed the crawling biters away from their exposed faces without urgency, ungloved. When they reached the netted garden enclosures, the ship walls curved up and out to left and right, warmed by the afternoon glow from Eder. Vlar opened the storm doors, and dragged the boxes of greens into the porch. When the doors were closed, she got out the squirters. She pulsed the bitter-smelling spray at Kan and Ajad, the two middle children, as they rotated slowly, hands over their eyes, and then she started on little Harr. The children shook out the supple folds of each other's suits, and worked their fingers through their cropped dark hair, feeling for the biters' carapaces. They mumbled through the squirting song. Vlar felt irritated going through the childish ritual.

Harr held the pan while Kan swept up the bodies. There were thirty-two biters and no other species, which Ajad noted carefully in the log. There never were any other species: Harr was adamant that the biters ate them all. They unzipped their outdoor suits and stowed them in the lockers, and threw their boots into the wallbin. Kan palmed open the corridor entrance for more ventilation, and the children sat at the old laboratory table on stools, and ate snap-peas. The insects murmured and rustled outside, the shadows of their crawling movement flickering across the porch's opaque ceiling panels.

"They're early this year." Kan glanced sideways at Ajad, always the one she needled first.

"It's only been three weeks since the berry bushes flowered. They shouldn't swarm yet." Ajad sounded anxious.

"I'll tell Hannit." Harr pushed himself off his stool one-handed and trotted down the corridor to the main body of the ship. The slapping of his feet echoed back against the increasingly unstable porch walls, built from repurposed ship-structure material many years ago. Vlar stood up, the uncompleted chores looming in her mind. She had to begin pilot training soon, to be any good, and still she was child-minding, housekeeping, wasting her time. She felt stifled in the gritty porch, and wanted to be in the clean control room, where she belonged.

"Time to clean these up." Vlar snapped open the cleanwater tap to fill the wide basin, and tipped her box of greens into the splashing water. Ajad fussed with the cords of the ceiling racks, and Kan took the first turn at swishing. The scent of the greens rose into the air, astringent and metallic. When the loose grit and frayed fibres had been washed off, Vlar clipped the green leaves efficiently into bundles, and Ajad hooked them onto the rack in rows.

As the first rack went up, the dripping greens sprinkled their heads and necks with cold drops. Kan yelped, and dashed to the shelter of the corridor. "Done my turn!" Vlar started working faster. Vanot and Borromit would be back from the fields soon, and she would need the sink clear for boll washing. She swished and clipped the bunches faster than Ajad could hang them, and the pile of clipped greens covered the table top.

"We never grow any leaves this big in the greenhouse," Ajad remarked. He swung the dripping second rack up, and pulled the third rack down.

"I could. I want to grow the biggest leaves and the heaviest fruit, but Hannit won't let me in the greenhouses." Vlar wondered why Kan was still harbouring a rejection from weeks ago, but she was distracted by a sensation in her face. Her bones were thrumming, a tiny vibration from nowhere. She rubbed her cool, damp hands over her cheeks.

The work on the ship seemed endless with so few people to do it. It had housed the Site One Settlement on Eder 4 for nine years, supplied by fertile earth, healthy fields, fresh water, fish from the sea and the luscious fruiting berries that grew near the burial ground. The cold volcano's bulk gave the Settlement protection from storms coming down from the north. But the ship had too many empty rooms. Vlar could not think of the dead crew by their names, not even her father, only their faces.

Harr came back up the corridor, taking light steps. His head was cocked, and he was looking into the corners of the wall panels and the floor. Then he pounced. Ajad shrieked, but Harr was an accurate hunter, and no biters were allowed indoors. They bit the adult crew, and sometimes made the children itch, and they ate anything they found. The half-crushed biter's legs were finger-length, and still twitching. "Big one," Harr said, with a wide smile. Kan offered him the pan and Harr carefully swept the body onto the scoop with a smooth sideswipe of his sleeve.

Vlar shoved the last clips of greens across the table to Ajad. She leaned back on her stool and looked at Harr with affection: he was such a sturdy, healthy, round little boy. She could remember when she seemed to be doing nothing but teach the children what to eat, what not to touch, how to do this, how not to do that. During the water plague she had kept them out of the way, so the dying could be nursed, and buried. The necrosis brought by the plague had created a horror of rotting limbs that rarely appeared now in her dreams. Harr had only lost his forearm. Kan had been too small to remember her parents dying one by one, and did not seem to care. Ajad had lost both parents at once, which was better. Vlar did not know when her mother would die, but she was waiting, braced. She braced herself a lot of the time.

Now that the children were learning and remembering what she taught them, they might have a chance. The unending feeling of responsibility for their lives was getting lighter as their self-sufficiency increased. Today she felt that they had turned a corner, crossed a line in a race for survival. Eder's warmth filled the room, and she stretched and flexed her toes. Her boots were tight, but there were plenty of spare sets. She would look for a larger pair. Pilots had to be comfortable.

The soft scream of a sled arriving rose above the insect murmur. Vlar had set the empty boxes ready beside the door, so Vanot could thrust the muddy fibre sacks of heavy, globular bolls straight into the boxes. But instead of greetings, Vanot's masked face showed no expression. As Kan pulled the first full box towards the sink, Vanot turned to pull in more sacks unloaded from the sled, keeping herself in the doorway to block the insects from getting in. The children dragged the boxes over the floor, but kept quiet. There was something unsaid in the room. Borromit must still be on the sled, but Vanot came indoors alone, the storm doors closing behind her. They could hear the insect murmur redoubling in the silence.

"He's gone, Vlar; he's gone." There was something wrong with Vanot's voice, it was abrupt with fatigue. Her face was grimy with windblown grey sand, and her eyes were red-rimmed. Her face mask was filthy.

"Where has he gone?" Ajad asked.

There was a pause. Vlar knew Vanot was talking to Nav. A drift of sand brushed past her feet as Vanot's heavy figure sagged to sit on a stool, her stormsuit and her outdoor boots dropping pieces of silvery dried pillak leaf onto the floor.

Vanot raised her eyes and looked at the children. "I'm sorry, Ajad. There was an accident. Borromit is dead. Hannit's coming." She bent to unfasten her boots. When she raised her head, the children saw tears running through the dust on her face. Vlar could hear their breathing getting faster. When she knelt down to help her mother with her boots, Vanot brought her head down to Vlar's shoulder and cried. Vlar put her arms around her. Harr ran back down the corridor towards the greenhouse.

When Vanot stood up to put her boots away, Hannit's shadow was moving rapidly up the corridor in the light from the open greenhouse doors. He arrived with Harr in his arms, Harr's face pressed to Hannit's thin neck. There was a pause. "Talking to Nav again," Vlar thought. "I wish I could do that. Will Nav cry like Vanot?'

"Why is Borromit dead?" Ajad said, glaring at Vanot now. "Why didn't you take us to help?'

Vanot struggled for patience. "Borromit was digging the insect dieoff into the furrows once we'd got the boll harvest out. It's heavy work. You're too small to help.'

Ajad howled. "I could have shovelled! You *said* we needed fertiliser!'

Vanot raised her hands in exasperation. "We had to work fast. The insects were rotting and swelling, too difficult to work unless you've got enough weight and strength. Borromit was shovelling them into the furrows as if there was no tomorrow." Her voice cracked and she swallowed. "He was delighted with it, good natural fertiliser, he said. We did six hours of work, no stopping, then he got tired very quickly. We could see the swarm coming, so we were in a hurry to get indoors. He turned the sled into the wind, by that outspur of the dune, and just fell over, and came off. Toppled. Like he'd lost his balance. I couldn't grab him. "

"I could have saved him! I would have held him on!" Rage made Ajad shout. His face was crumpled and red, and he ran out of the porch down the corridor, Kan following.

Vanot was talking to Hannit, more quietly. "When I got hold of the sled controls and turned it around, Borromit was on the ground, and the swarm was coming towards us from the sea. I could see its mottled shadow. You know the way it thickens and swells when it begins the descent. I flew the sled back as fast as I could, to get Borromit off the ground, but his face was covered in the things and they were ripping his hands apart." Her voice was uncertain, as if she could not believe what she had seen.

Hannit stood rigid. His voice was horrified. "They've never done that before. Was he still alive?"

"No. No blood. He must have had a heart attack. Or broke his neck in the fall. He was already dead when they got to him." Her voice cracked, and she gulped in a sob, throwing her head back angrily.

Harr's head lifted from Hannit's shoulder, listening, and he looked towards the table at the back of the porch. One of the sacks had slumped and was moving.

Vanot looked round when she heard the movement, and wiped her face with the strip of old undershirt from her pocket. "It's just a boll, Harr. They're round, and fall over, make the sack unstable."

"Not a boll. There're more biters. There's something else there too." Harr sagged to make his father let him down, still watching the sacks. He moved towards the porch doorway.

"More insects," Vlar said. "We can hear 'em."

"Something else," Harr repeated.

Hannit looked around the porch walls, and handed Vanot the second squirter. He pulled on a pair of outdoor gloves left on the table. Vanot pulled hers back on. Vlar took Harr's hand and stepped back to the corridor entrance, her other hand on the door control.

"They're coming out. Close the door, Vlar," Vanot said, looking carefully at the sacks on the table. "Full seal." Hannit was checking the squirter level, and Vanot had pulled her hood back up.

"They don't hurt us," Vlar said again, but Vanot wasn't listening, and the door closed. Through the door window Vlar watched her mother and Hannit methodically destroying the insects that were emerging from the boll sacks.

"Hungry," Harr remarked. He'd lost interest in the sack when the door had closed.

"It's not meal-time yet," Vlar replied, peering through the window, her toes stretched. It was still a little too high for her to see through easily. Harr walked down the corridor towards the sleeping-rooms.

Hannit had cleared and emptied four sacks, and Vanot was poking the fifth, when it leaped upwards, like an attacking finfish erupting from the sea. The sack seemed to shred in the air, stray insects fluttering out of the rents in the old fibrecloth, and a heavy, black-furred moler tumbled back to the table. It was blind but sharp-toothed and the acidic edges of its mouthparts showed a livid yellowy grey. Hannit jerked backwards, his hand at his waist and his squirter rolling on the floor, but Vanot's weapon was already out of its holder, making a familiar, hissing drone.

The insects were frizzled, the moler lay seeping, in two pieces, and the sack was beyond repair. Hannit poked the remnants cautiously with his own weapon. Nothing moved. Vlar opened the connecting door to a smell of cooked meat. She switched the ventilation on again, and its labouring vibration blended with the thrumming of the insects outside. Vanot smiled at her, but Vlar could still see the marks of tears down her mother's dusty face.

"Horrible." Hannit was scraping the bodies into the pan, and gave it to Vanot. She walked down the corridor towards the waste disposal section. He finished stowing the suits, gloves, squirters and boots, and looked around, and up at the drying racks. "Good crop. You always leave the porch in good order, Vlar. Everything always where it should be. You and the children are a credit to the crew. Thank you.'

Vlar was pleased, but wanted the ventilation to work faster. The curved porch walls seemed uncomfortably thin against the thrumming noise outside. Were they vibrating too? "Was it inside one of the bolls?'

'Probably. It must have been asleep after eating, and then it was harvested.'

Vlar faltered. "What do we do about Borromit?"

Hannit sat down at the table where the emptied sacks were folded, and clasped his hands. His natural paleness seemed intensified. "We should talk to Nav about it, but we can't do anything until we know the swarm has gone. The wind might drive them away, but it'll be dark soon. Tomorrow, Vanot will look for his body, and bury him. She can't do anything now.'

Vlar moved away from the thought of Borromit, and his poor hands, his poor face. They had work to do. She could help properly now. "I need a shiplink to be able to talk to Nav," she said. "You and Vanot aren't enough now.'

Hannit attempted a smile. "Nav thinks so too.'

There had to be at least three at the Settlement to tell Nav what to do when Nav couldn't make the decisions. The doors had to open and close, the ventilation had to cycle, the waste had to compost, and the water had to be clean. Vlar wasn't sure what she could tell Nav to do that wasn't in the program, but she did want a shiplink.

"We need to talk to Myennit," Vanot said, walking back into the porch, carrying the empty pan. "I need a clean shipsuit, Vlar.'

"I put it on your bunk after you went out this morning," Vlar said reprovingly. If she was going to have a shiplink, she wanted to be part of crew conversations, and not be shunted off the deck when it mattered.

"Oh Vlar," and Vanot's voice faltered. She looked up at the ceiling and her voice sounded thick. "Borromit always said you were the quartermaster any captain would die for."

Vlar did not like it when the adults talked about dying. She wanted to talk to Nav. She wanted to get buried in scheduling routines and shipboard checks. She did not want to think about Borromit.

"I need to be able to talk to Nav. Hannit said so, and Nav too.'

Hannit nodded. "We also have to contact Myennit. Once Vlar has the link, she can raise Backup at Site Two. Might take some time. Are you ready, Vlar?"

In the control room, Vanot recorded a formal report for transmission. Nav acknowledged, and requested that Vlar be given third-access duties. Vlar grinned nervously. She had known Nav all her life, but she had never had the direct link, only basic audio. And now she was to get a full shiplink, full communication with all systems, and Site Two, and the satellite, and the relay ship to Home, and the stars! Her heart was thumping, and her palms felt sweaty.

Vanot hoisted her up to the console so Nav could rescan her eyes, fingers, face and voice for the record. She shuffled backwards off the work surface to the console chair, Borromit's old chair, and hooked herself up to audio so Nav could give her a basic rapid-induct while running a baseline biosynthesis to update her ship records. After fifty minutes Vlar had drained the cup of water that Vanot had left for her, and was hungry again. Nav must have called Vanot back, because she returned to the control room while Vlar was unhooking. She gave Vlar a boll-noodle roll on a plate, but was looking puzzled.

"Nav says there's a block on third-access for you. I don't understand why that's there, so I'll have to delete it manually. Some override Myennit might know about. Borromit would have known.'

"Who set it?" Vlar was outraged. Why was she blocked?

Vanot was keying and swiping rapidly. "No sign. Oh, yes. It's an external.'

"Specialists! Those Specialists," Vlar was almost shouting, but she pulled her anger back. Vanot continued keying. "No evidence that it's them, but probably, yes. Done. Nav can clear you now."

Vlar was enraged, engulfed by a familiar upswelling of anger that she hadn't felt since she'd run away from the Specialists. "Why did they block me?'

'Probably more exposure restrictions, though I don't see why. Third-access doesn't endanger you any more than no access. They had an interfering attitude." Vanot cleaned her hands and swabbed Vlar's neck and scalp. *"Put the plate away. Have you calmed down now? Hold steady. One prick, and there you go. That's my girl."* Her voice sounded fond and proud, but her face was serious. She inserted the needle into the vein behind Vlar's ear, and Nav sent in the bloodbot. Vlar knew that it would anchor somewhere between her ear and the top of her skull, and waited. She didn't feel anything, barely even the pressure of the needle in her vein. Nav opened the connection and Vlar gasped.

*"Nav!"* Through her shiplink she continued (I hear/see/feel you!).

(This is good, Vlar. I hear/feel you too.) Nav replied. Vlar grinned widely at her mother, and Vanot left the room.

(Hannit wants me to contact Myennit.) Vlar told Nav.

(Initiated. Wait for the confirmation signal, then key the message to Backup. Keep it within one despatch. You should explain clearly. Myennit must know about Borromit, and be reminded that Settlement is below crew limits.)

Vlar hesitated, her hand over the keypad, then she drew her hands back. (What will Backup already know?)

(Backup cannot read your mind. You must give the right information to be fully understood.)

But Vlar felt aggrieved, as a thought occurred to her.

(Why don't I count as crew yet?)

(You are under fifteen years, so legally you are a child. It has been noted that you have functioned as an adult for two years and three months. But there is a point in your physiological development that must be passed. A child is dependent on parental input, as an infant depends on the maternal immunities in its blood to protect it while its own immunities are developing. When you have passed that point, you are adult. Your biochemistry determines when the adaptation point has been passed.)

Vlar was awestruck: Nav had never said so much to her before. But, adaptation?

(What immunities? To the biters?)

(To this planet's biota, its atmospheric components, its radiation, its magnetic field. All contribute to your development as your bones grow and your brain develops. The Specialists study this.)

Nav changed its tone, and a subtle urgency infused Vlar's mind.

(Myennit needs to return. Send Backup the data so she may make an informed decision.)

Vlar keyed the message, striving for formal succinctness and the warmth of affectionate need. Although Backup would not appreciate her efforts, she wanted something of herself to come through the pulses of energy flashing through the distances. She thought about the cross-planet communications string. Far above in the vacuum, the ship's tiny comms satellite was hurtling through its planetary orbit, bristling with antennae and receptors. Vlar's signal pinged up, and down, up and down, calling out to Site Two, on the southern continent, on the other side of the sea. Backup would tell Myennit at once when her message arrived. She slid down from the console chair. Nav would let her know when Myennit answered.

She felt elated. She could talk to Nav, and Nav could tell her if anything needed doing. Nav was a new person to talk to about Ajad and Kan and their fights and silences, about Harr getting heavier, about how to fix clothes that didn't fit, and the screeching whine in the greywater tap. She could talk to Nav about maths and classes and exploring and riding the sled, and how, exactly, the insects had killed Borromit and what it had felt like and would it happen to anyone else. Vlar's mind was buzzing.


In the morning, Nav did not wake her, and there was no message from Myennit. Vlar climbed back onto her seat at the console.

(Good morning Nav.) Did Nav like to be greeted?

(Good morning Vlar.) She didn't have anything else to ask. She hoped she hadn't interrupted anything. Did Nav chat, she wondered.

Vlar ran through some shipchecks to explore her new accesses. She looked up the maintenance log for the greywater tap, and decided that it needed grease and reassembly. Nav agreed that this was a sensible approach. She would find the grease in porch locker 5.

She couldn't hear anyone else moving in the ship yet.

(Has Vanot gone out?)

(Yes. She left with the sled at 05.75.)

Vlar wondered if the sled had been set to recharge overnight. She did some maths, then climbed down to ask Hannit about breakfast. Hannit was in the greenhouse, tying up tendrils and planting out the new seedlings for winter crops. He was preoccupied, working fast, and told Vlar to see to the food for the day. His voice was agitated, and Vlar slid out silently. She looked in the stores. When Ajad and Kan came to eat, Hannit told them stories about plants and fungus infections, but Vlar could see that he was thinking about something else. Harr slept late.

When Vlar began to disassemble the greywater tap, she had to switch on the porch light because so little was coming through the ceiling panels. Clouds seemed to be passing over the ship very low. Vlar realised that she had assimilated the sounds of the biters into the usual outdoor sounds. Their continuous humming drone resonated oddly with the bones in her face. She pressed her fingers to her cheeks, then below the back of her skull. No difference.

When she was cranking the tap shut again, Harr came to her, wanting to play, so Vlar put away her tools and the grease. They played tunnels and molers, Harr shrieking with laughter, and then she read him a story. Vanot was still out. Hannit said that she was finishing the harvest, but Vlar knew that she was looking for Borromit. Vlar read more stories to the children. She mended the broken bed-leg that rocked annoyingly by taking the screw out and redoing it. She hadn't been able to tighten it completely last time she was in charge of disassembly drill, and now she did it without thinking.

There were too many insects outdoors to send the children out to work in the garden or to play. They played in the corridor instead, running and jumping, thumping the walls and floor with happy yelps.

'I'm the swarm!'

'I'm Myennit!'

'I'm Backup, covered in biters,' and Harr crawled on the ground, twitching mechanically.

'I'm Myennit squirting the biters!' Kan aimed and shrieked wildly.

'I'm the swarm! I will eat you!' and Ajad ran howling at the other two, who yelled and ran for their beds.

Vlar went to the control room and closed the door. She began to explore her new access, that led her to new records, the scheduled reports to Home (she had never seen these before), the stores assessments, her own files from birth, and the Specialists' reports. Vlar read these hungrily, and found she was kneeling up in the console chair to see the screen more closely.

Nav made no remark, but a ping from the console room hatch broke her stunned reverie. She made herself focus on the hot drink Nav had sent her, sipping with care, sitting upright on her seat, legs dangling. She peered at the skin on her free hand, held her arm up to the light and turned it, studying the bone length. She put the drink down and felt with both hands at the back of her head the familiar nodes under the curve of her skull, which she had had as long as she could remember. She squinted at the walls, wondering for the first time what colours she was seeing. Would her eyes still pass for a pilot's even after adaptation?


Vlar began putting the midday meal together while she waited for Vanot. She heard Hannit go into the control room, and then go straight to the porch to begin suiting up. Vlar followed him, startled. Hannit had not left the ship in years.

'I'm taking the second sled to bring Vanot back. Her sled is out of power.' Vlar stared at him. His voice was jumpy, and he fumbled with the suit seals. When Vlar handed him his face mask, he fastened it wrongly, then did it again. He chattered about nothing, saying stupid things about leaves and soil, and looked nervously out of the window while adjusting his gloves.

The insect murmur was steady. He was looking up at the ceiling panels where the moving shadows patrolled. 'I don't want them to follow me. I'll keep the hood up, fly out to sea first, then double round.'

Vlar shouted silently at Nav. (Nav! Can Hannit remember how to fly?)

(He has retrained since the crew numbers reduced.)

Hannit stepped through the storm doors, his feet crunching on the sand, and the doors slammed closed. Vlar realised that he had forgotten how light the doors weighed, and how strong the wind was. She heard the remaining sled whine up in power, and then whirl away through a fuzz of reverberating insect drone.

The sled had lights, and infrared, and they could stay out all night in it. Vanot would be fine: she had done long trips by sled and it carried everything she would need. She and Hannit would come back together, and Borromit would have been buried properly. Vanot was waiting to be collected, sitting in the sled, safe from biters. Nav knew what was happening. Everyone would be fine. Vlar went back to the kitchen, and carefully made an extra stew that would be there for reheating by anyone who was hungry.

In the afternoon Vlar sat at the console, and looked again at her data. Harr came to play a game on another screen, and curled up to sleep in the enclosing chair. When he woke up, Vlar called Ajad and Kan in to watch a story. When it was finished the ship was still. Vlar wondered if she were acclimatising to the insect sounds. She could no longer hear them. Her face felt normal.

(Nav: turn on external vision, please.)

(Initiated.)

Vlar touched the screen and saw the view outside, as if she were raised above the porch door. She turned the viewer 360 degrees, and saw nothing that should not be there, saw nothing that was not familiar. The visibility seemed quite good, so the insects had moved on. Where were they?

(Nav: has Hannit found Vanot yet?)

(The sleds are not within range. Hannit is not tagged.) Vlar's mouth opened in shock. What had Hannit been thinking of, to go out without a link? Did he even think of it? Why hadn't she noticed?

(Where did he go?)

(Hannit operated a drone at 10.37. It returned at 11.15.)

(Send it out again, following the same route.)

Vlar opened up the external visual again, and waited for Nav to patch her into dronesight. The visual wavered as the drone rose out of the port, and steadily moved north towards the pillak trees. Some dark flurries passed across her view. The land miniaturised as the drone ascended towards the spindly trunks and whipping rhizomes of the pillak trees. Nav took the drone around the summit of the dunes, making a wide circuit, and then moved down the slope on the other side.

A sled stood parked beside the burial ground, its lights dead. There was no one visible, no one moving. Vlar peered for the sled's markings.

(Is that Vanot's sled?)

(Yes. It should be retrieved for recharging.)

(Can you detect Vanot?)

Another, very brief pause. (There is no connection.)

Vlar pushed her panic back into her stomach. She breathed hard, and pushed her back against the seat. It made her feet stick out in front, but she wanted the chair wrapped around her.

(Vlar, the drone should return in 23 minutes.)

(Bring it back past the trees on the other side. I want to see round there.)

The drone rose and moved smoothly towards the great dune ridge, and she could see the cone of the cold volcano on her left. There was movement in the sky above the trees.

(Nav! Stop! There's the sled!)

Vlar said this aloud in her excitement, and she heard the children coming into the control room. They were bored without her, and curious about the visuals they could see on the big screen. Harr climbed into his father's chair.

The sled had overturned completely. They could see its numbers on its base, and a jagged crack across the hull. Vlar peered desperately, looking for the orange stormsuits. A whizzing flash of movement passed beneath the dronesight.

(Nav: get the drone above the range of the whippers, but increase magnification.)

The drone moved upwards at speed, and then the ground and the cracked hull rushed towards her again. Vlar saw movement beneath the hull. An arm appeared around the side, it flapped at them.

"Hannit wants us to go away," Kan said, unexpectedly. 'He does that when he's shouting at me in the greenhouse.'

Ajad and Harr were staring at the screen, and Vlar saw Hannit's arm emerge again. There was a convulsive lurch as the hull slid further down the hill. Hannit came into view grabbing at the hull to pull it back up the slope, and Vlar caught sight of a second orange suit, lying under where the hull had been, pressed into the sand, with something wrong about its arrangement of legs and arms. Hannit's legs were hidden.

(Vlar: the drone must return soon.)

As Vlar was staring at the screen, and Harr was beginning to wail, the screen filled with reddish-black movement and the drone's horizontals lurched.

(Bring it back!) Vlar shrieked silently. (Bring it home!)

The drone's visuals rushed up to the slope of the dune, over the top of a pillak tree and down towards the ship, which grew rapidly in size. The drone's visual cut out as it hovered above its docking port. The last scene, frozen on the screen, was of a grey, sandy beach, empty and clean, with grey waves in a grey sea.

(Nav: the swarm has got them, hasn't it?)

(Yes.)

(It's eating them, isn't it?)

(I will be with you, Vlar. I will help you.)

"Where is Hannit, Vlar?" Kan was looking straight at her, and her voice was high-pitched and strained.

Vlar paused.

(Nav: help me!)

She looked at the children. "They won't be coming back. They had an accident. They're dead." The children looked at her, and back at the screen.

"Did Nav say so?'

"Yes. Nav is helping us. We'll be safe with the AI." Vlar wondered if 'he' or 'her' were right for Nav, but couldn't think of the right words just now.

After some time had passed, Kan turned her head as she heard the familiar sound of the storyteller switching on. She uncurled from Vlar's lap, and Harr went with her to sit down in front of the screen, and Ajad followed. Vlar half-heard the storyteller going through the long story of adventure and loss and excitement, and saw the children curl up on the floor as they settled into the familiar rhythms and words. She dozed, dimly aware that Nav was making her sleepy, and she felt warm.

When Vlar woke, she drove herself to do tasks. When she had reheated the stew, and made the children eat, and read more stories, and had seen them into bed and had cleared the kitchen, and checked the greenhouse schedules, Vlar went back to the control room. She was crying now with shock and tiredness, and went to sleep in her console chair. When she awoke, feeling chilly and stiff, she went to her own bed, and slept for the whole night. She fell asleep feeling bereft beyond anything that stories had prepared her for. The winds rose and fell.

In the morning, Vlar wrote out a jobs list and set Ajad and Kan to their schoolwork. When they were preoccupied she looked again outside the ship on external visual. There were no insects, and Eder was warming the air strongly. She felt her nodes and nothing was changed. Everything had changed.

(Nav: what shall we do?)

(I will help you look after the children until Myennit returns. She will decide what to do about Hannit and Vanot.)

Vlar clamped down on fear. She would make lists, she would not forget anything and she would work hard. Ajad would keep the log. Kan would work in the greenhouse where she always wanted to be anyway. Harr would learn to read as well as he could count and they would all do the cooking. Myennit would come back and find the ship working and the crew in good order.

Eder continued to shine. In mid-afternoon, Nav interrupted her ferocious work in the garden.

(Vlar. Backup is in contact. Myennit wants to speak to you. I've reported about Hannit and Vanot.)

Vlar slammed the storm doors shut and ran into the control room. She was crying with relief. She scrambled into her chair, gasping for breath, her face all wet and heated, and tumbled out her story to Myennit's pale face on the screen. "And Kan is fine, she's in the greenhouse," she finished. Myennit would want to know about Kan above all others. "When are you coming home, Myennit?" She was mopping her eyes and nose, and her breath was ragged.

Myennit was speaking. "Vlar, I know. Thank you, thank you. My poor Hannit. And Vanot." She paused, and turned her head briefly away from the screen.

"We're coming back to Settlement. Site Two is going to complicate things." Her face was tense, and a tear track stained her cheek, but, there was a suppressed tone of excitement in her voice. "We think the biters are the sentient species. We've found structures here, ritual features. We have to activate the first contact protocols, then leave the area. We need to plan to withdraw from the mission, in case the sentients don't want our presence." She paused. "This is what Bottomlt, Vanot, all of us hoped for. But the biters! That was not anticipated. We may be going Home, Vlar." Her tone was aching: they would have to leave the dead.

"But I can't leave," Vlar began to say. "That's why the Specialists left early, before they started adapting. And if you've got adaptations too…" But Myennit was speaking again.

"I'm worried about the biters' attacks at Settlement. They seem deliberate, and out of pattern. What did Vanot," and here Myennit remembered visibly that she was speaking to Vlar about her dead mother, "what did Vanot do with the mounds of insect dieoff, in the fields?'

'They dug them into the old furrows.'

Myennit glanced upwards, as if looking through the tiny ceiling port of her sled. "Vlar, we mustn't touch them again. Those mounds may have been their burial grounds.'

Suddenly Vlar did not feel safe. What if the insects had changed their minds about her, and the children? Would their immunity still work? Myennit's tone changed, she spoke briskly, with command.

"We're leaving here as fast as we can, pulling out now. You and the children must stay indoors. I will tell Nav what to do." She was looking directly at Vlar, and smiled once with a forced expression, then her screen blanked.

Vlar pulled up the external visual, and looked southward. A new dark mass was visible, on the edge of the horizon, heading out across the narrow sea. Vlar punched in a message to Nav, to let Myennit know that the swarm was on its way. Her face was thrumming again. She knew Myennit was telling Nav how to bridge the gap between inexperience and survival, how to get them past the adaptation point. But Myennit would come back, Vlar was certain.

She looked out of the console room, and could see Eder's light coming in through the porch window. It was warming the room, making the solar collectors hum gently. If they had power, they had Nav, they had stores, they had water. They were adapted, they would adapt. The biters would leave them alone because they were adapted. This was her home.

Kate Macdonald is a literary historian and publisher, from Aberdeen in NE Scotland. She lives near Bath, in Somerset, halfway up a hill. Deer tromp past her washing line and eat the windfalls.

# Last Words

## Laura Duerr

**I** **'d anticipated wearing my dress grays** for the first time at my graduation. I was supposed to have been the first Garissite to become an Alliance officer; instead, I was attending my mentor's funeral and facing expulsion.

I stood with the other second-year cadets, all human, while we waited for the instructors and visiting Alliance officers to take their seats behind General Terrick's black-draped coffin. My collar was too snug and it pressed sharp-edged against my throat, which was already taut with tears I wouldn't shed. I tried to keep my attention on the music – mournful strings from the General's homeworld – but it was hard to ignore the cadets whispering behind me.

"She's out for sure, now." Rani Walthis, granddaughter of General Walthis, who'd wanted me gone since I enrolled. She'd spent my entire first year seeking any kind of excuse to dismiss me, but I gave her none, presenting myself flawlessly at every surprise inspection, passing every test, and pushing my physical fitness until I was outpacing third-years.

"She's not worthy of those pins." Jeph, eldest son of House Antwe.

My fingers twitched, wanting to sign in retaliation: *I earned them!* The polished silver bars gleamed on my shoulders. I was top of our class: Terrick always told me they resented my success. The Human-Garissi War had ended before I was born, but its legacy was fresh in the memories of both the Alliance and Garisst. My becoming an officer would symbolize peace and unity and pave the way for more non-human worlds to join the Alliance. Some believed I'd been given the pins out of pity, or to push some political agenda. When anyone pointed out that my excellent grades more than qualified me, that was excused away, too.

"What made Terrick pick *her*, anyway?" Rani again. "Do you think she made Elite?"

"Maybe that's why she did it." The whisper was either Mari or Sanessa – both were fourth-years, bright and cunning, but lazy. "Terrick recommended her, so Bree got what she wanted..."

"Doesn't need her anymore," Jeph agreed.

"If Terrick is dead, do her picks still count?" Alliance nepotism might have gotten Rani into the Academy, but so far she'd failed to sufficiently impress her grandmother. Rani couldn't be bothered by what may or may not have happened to Terrick – all she wanted was to make Elite, ideally instead of me.

"Not just dead, *murdered*. Bree doesn't stand a chance now." Jeph's undisguised satisfaction burned in my ears – not just because he hated me, but because he might be right.

My fingers danced: *Yes, I do.*

Maybe the cadets saw me sign, maybe they didn't; regardless, they fell silent. They had picked up some Garissite signing over the years, whether they wanted it or not. They certainly never stooped to using it. When I first came to the Academy, the instructors made me answer everything in writing. General Terrick had been the first to learn signing, and she'd lobbied to have translation software added to Academy shuttles and simulations so I could use my primary chirping language and keep my hands free for flying. It was thanks to her I'd been able to fly at all.

Now she was gone, her death tied to my supposed negligence. General Walthis had been injured too, when our shuttle crashed into her observation deck. It truly was an accident, but on that, they had only the word of a Garissite against General Walthis herself. The result was inevitable.

But Terrick had helped me one last time. The Academy could ignore my grades, but they couldn't ignore her final words. I just needed the chance to let her speak them.

The strings ceased, the final chord reverberating through the Hall of Faiths, leaving empty stone arches in its wake. I hated how gray it all was – gray stone walls looming over gray uniforms – and I knew Terrick would have hated it, too. She liked – *had* liked – bright colors, in art and flowers and food. I'd taught her to paint in exchange for additional political science tutoring, and she'd been the only human I knew who understood that the Garissi also spoke in color, that a painting could tell a different story by changing a shade of green; that, on Garisst, our omnipresent screens contextualized our chirps and hisses with the hues of our emotions made physical on our chests. Her first clumsy paintings portrayed uncomplicated emotions in cheerful ochre, bright cerulean, or undiluted violet. Later, they became more sophisticated: muted reds paired with warm grays to indicate the stress of leadership; her childhood memories captured in candy-bright pinks and blues against wistful navy.

And now she lay under impassive black.

She'd have hated this.

A sergeant stood and called for attention. Thousands of boot heels met in a snap like a gunshot and I couldn't help flinching.

General Walthis and the Tethos sector governor marched onto the stage, saluted the Alliance flag, and took their seats. Walthis' eye was still bandaged. I felt the now-familiar flash of green-tinged bitterness that the crash that had killed Terrick had barely grazed Walthis.

Terrick had been all that stood between me and obscurity. I needed to make Elite by my third year or I'd be sent home. My fall wouldn't be immediate, and it wouldn't be evident to anyone other than me, but the signs would be there: my grades would begin to drop, no matter how hard I studied; I'd rack up demerits for having a scratched button or asymmetrical boot laces; more shuttle issues and simulation glitches would eat away at my compulsory flight hours. Without the very public honor of Elite status to protect me, eventually Walthis or someone else would find an excuse to quietly expel me. And that was without rumors of murder hanging over me.

Headmaster Tern took the stage. "We are gathered in memory of General Alarra Terrick of Tethos..."

Later I couldn't recall what any of them had said. They each talked for what felt like hours. Only when her nephew stood to ritually collect her spirit for safe return to Tethos did a lone tear creep down my cheek.

I could choose to break formation to brush it away, but whether I did or not, the story would be that I wept for my mentor, that I wasn't officer material, that I was useless without Terrick. I wasn't qualified to make Elite, let alone graduate – so much for the Garissi then.

Better than the alternative, that I was a remorseless killer who couldn't be bothered to feign grief, even at the funeral. Maybe they'd actually believe me now – but I suspected that until I played the recording in my breast pocket, no amount of weeping would change any minds.

Regardless, I shed no more tears.


After the funeral came the cliques, and the sideways glances, and the lowered voices. I circled the Hall, keeping watch for

Headmaster Tern. No one offered condolences. The human string quartet continued to play placid songs, nothing unsuitable, but nothing really beautiful, either.

They'd put one of her paintings on display. They probably thought it simply pretty, a representation of Terrick's well-roundedness and talent. To a Garissite, though, the technical quality was secondary to her color choices, which spoke of hope, unity, and repentance.

I stood at-ease studying it. She'd completed it just a couple months ago. The swirls of pale blue and peach danced across the hard olive and steel background that signified our peoples' troubled past. It was the first one she'd done without asking me for advice on the colors.

"It'll be on the stage when you graduate," Terrick had said when she showed me the finished painting. "We'll tell them, together, what it means."

My eyes traced every brush stroke, every shift in shade, seeking clues that weren't there. I could guess at what it meant, but Terrick's original meaning was gone now. And I still needed to convey her other message before it was too late for both of us. Headmaster Tern was my best option there, but after nearly half an hour of mingling, it was becoming increasingly apparent that he was avoiding me.

I remained patient. Only once did someone try to beat me up. I'd slipped into the restrooms for the fourth time, seeking refuge from the press of all those stares, but Cadet Alma and her bench-press-record-holding friends followed me in. I carefully protected the pins on my shoulders, but instead I lost a uniform button and tore one of the pockets. They left me to stop up my bleeding nostrils over the sink. The button I found rolled under one of the toilets; I reattached it with the sewing kit I kept tucked in my boot. The torn pocket was easy to fix, too. Miraculously, not a single drop of my purplish blood had landed on my grays. A bloody uniform would have earned me my first demerit, and started the countdown on my remaining time at the Academy.

I straightened my jacket, confirmed that the recording was intact, and returned to the Hall.

There, at last, was Tern, alone. I intercepted him.

"Cadet Bree," he said civilly. "My sympathies for your loss."

*Thank you*, I signed. *I need your help.*

"Help? With what?"

*The crash investigation is ongoing, yes? I have evidence.*

He looked around as if checking for eavesdroppers. "What kind of evidence? Why didn't you turn it in?"

Because I'd been in shock for hours after, because I didn't know who I could trust, because it was all I had left of her.

*I wanted to give it directly to you. I was afraid of it being* – I hesitated, trying to decide on the best sign – *lost.*

He nodded. "You're being interviewed again tomorrow. We'll look into it then."

A flash of panic, scarlet. *By whom?*

"Military police. Just some clarifying questions, nothing to worry about."

Military police had already questioned me about the accident, as had the school and an Alliance oversight committee. They'd even brought in a Garissite interrogator, an experience I'd actually slightly enjoyed because it was the first face-to-face conversation I'd had with another Garissite in months, utilizing our full range of vocalizations and color displays. All my responses had been recorded and analyzed. If the Alliance wanted to question me again, it meant either they didn't believe me, or didn't want to and needed a concrete reason to convict me. If I gave even one unsatisfactory answer at this stage, I could be held indefinitely. Forget expulsion – I'd stand trial for sabotage and murder.

*Now!* I signed, pleading.

But Tern frowned. "I simply don't have time at the moment. You understand." He gestured to the crowds. "Your interview is at 0800 tomorrow – we can discuss it then."

And he left.

My fingers fluttered anxiously. The investigation was moving too slowly to satisfy the school board, Alliance bureaucrats, and Tethos authorities who were all clamoring for answers. The

Academy didn't want to admit to their fatal maintenance error, and factions of the Alliance would welcome an excuse to keep their ranks closed to non-humans. My people might even be grateful to the Alliance for not viewing my supposed 'attack' as a Garissite act of war.

My silver honor pins didn't matter. Terrick's recommendations didn't matter. I'd make a convenient, tidy scapegoat.

Not for the first time, I wondered if the shuttle had been rigged, if I'd been framed. That kind of speculation was useless, though. I had evidence that would clear my name regardless of the true cause of the crash – I just needed someone to trust me. Apparently that someone wasn't Tern.

The human string quartet was still playing bland human songs. The triteness of the music made me want to splash crimson rage over everything in sight. Every minute that passed was a lost opportunity, but if I approached just one wrong person, had just one sign misconstrued, that would be the end.

Very few of the other ranking Academy personnel knew enough signing for me to communicate something of this magnitude. I only had one more person who might be able – and willing – to help me. I hadn't approached her before because of judicial rules, but I was rapidly running out of both options and time.

Chaplain DeNaar had given the closing benediction at Terrick's funeral. Her position was uniquely challenging in that she had to provide spiritual support for at least five major faiths that coexisted at the Academy, but she also held one of the few positions that allowed total confidentiality. Therapists and counselors could be ordered to disclose transcripts; conversations with the chaplain remained secret. If I talked to her within the sanctity of the Hall, I should be doubly secure.

I waited at a polite distance while she prayed with another student, a young man struggling to hold back tears. At the conclusion of the prayer, he looked up, saw me, and frowned. He left quickly, even while I attempted to sign my condolences to him.

Chaplain DeNaar smiled sympathetically. "Ando was scheduled for a training mission like yours this week. It's hitting him rather hard."

*The General was a great teacher,* I signed. *We will all miss her.*

"You especially, I'm guessing."

She said it without rancor, but I still felt black and olive spikes of grief and shame.

*I keep hoping my grades will speak for me.*

"I don't think anyone here can argue you're a poor student."

*But?* I signed before I could stop myself.

She shifted, uncomfortable. "But...General Walthis provided a very clear account of what happened to the shuttle. There might be consequences for you."

*Do you think I killed her?* Signing was often blunt. I didn't bother to soften the question.

She looked appropriately startled. "Of course not! It was a tragic accident. Once the investigation concludes, the truth will come out and the furor will die down."

'Furor' was a polite way to describe 'threats and assault', but I let it go. *What if I had proof it was an accident? Would you help me?*

I expected her to agree obliquely, to suggest that I return to the Hall of Faiths again later in order to fill her in privately. Instead, she shook her head.

"Cadet, I cannot get involved in legal matters, you know that."

*I'm in danger if I don't get help.*

"What kind of help do you need that the school or the MPs can't provide?"

*A witness. I have a recording from the shuttle.*

DeNaar shook her head emphatically. "Anything of the sort should have been turned in to the authorities."

Again, the assumption that human authorities would look impartially on my evidence with galactic politics looming over their shoulders. *I didn't think it was safe.*

"Cadet," she said, gently but with the all-too-familiar tone of patronization creeping in, "this makes it look like you have something to hide. If you want my help, let me give you some advice: cooperate with the investigation. Let it take its course. If you're innocent, you have nothing to worry about."

I twitched my fingers, half-formed thoughts reaching my hands before I could cohere them. She squinted, trying to interpret my fluttering, until I finally held my palms up flat – no more to say.

*Thank you,* I said brusquely. And I strode away.

Had she even noticed my swollen nostrils? Did she not hear, or was she ignoring, the whispers that followed in my wake? Did she not keep a running tally of how many people called me murderer, how many of my fellow cadets and even instructors expected, if not outright anticipated, my expulsion?

I spotted Headmaster Tern again, conferring with the sector governor and Captain Fassil of the military police, who had overseen my interviews. Tern looked away quickly when he saw me watching, and Fassil excused himself. The sector governor had a thick beard, making his expression unreadable to me. Facial hair wasn't allowed in the military, so I had less practice interpreting human emotion when the face was obscured like his was. Would he be willing to help me?

"Cadet Bree."

I snapped to attention at the sound of a cool female voice. *General. Ma'am.*

General Walthis barely bothered to conceal her triumphant smile. "I've just heard a rumor of brawling in the restrooms. Does this explain your slovenly appearance?"

I knew there was no point in trying to explain I'd been assaulted, that I hadn't even fought back, so I feigned misunderstanding. *Ma'am. My dress grays haven't been properly fitted since I wasn't supposed to need them for another two years.*

"You mean at your graduation."

I signed a slightly defiant assent.

"Your top button is not aligned correctly. A witness tells me that button came detached during your fight."

*I tried to sew it back—*

"Unsatisfactory appearance warrants a demerit, but that is the least of your concerns, Cadet. Brawling, especially with an older student like Cadet Alma, is a much more serious disciplinary matter."

She leaned close and I resisted flinching. I hoped she couldn't tell how quick my respiration had become.

"I know you had something to do with Terrick's death, Cadet." She whispered it like a curse. Over her shoulder, I saw the sector governor give Tern a farewell handshake and my heart sank. "Your behavior tonight just confirms that you are violent, just like the rest of your people, and I will not tolerate it any longer. As soon as you leave this building, you're mine."

I remained at attention long after she'd strode away. I could almost forgive how Walthis projected her prejudice against the Garissi on me – her first husband had died in the war, and loss lingers – and I could even overlook her regressive desire for a human-only Alliance. And I'd endured her personal grudge, hoping to simply prove her wrong by accomplishing my goals, but advocating for my academic failure was one thing: conspiring against my very freedom was something else.

The vast gray Hall felt small and stifling.

Fine – if everyone wanted me to go to the military police, I'd show the captain here and now. Apparently I'd be seeing him soon, one way or another.

Fassil was donning his helmet, preparing to leave. I followed after him as quickly as I could without drawing attention, pushing through the heavy glass doors of the Hall out onto the broad front steps. The stars hung cold and still in the black overhead. Cool white street lamps kept the area bright, and the pale concrete Academy buildings around us gleamed like monuments. A row of shuttles and cabs waited at the foot of the steps to transport guests. A few clusters of MP shuttles dotted the periphery. Pairs of officers stood here and there along the steps and walkways – but somehow Captain Fassil had already disappeared.

A pair of shuttles took off, their taillights leaving red trails through the night. I squinted at the remaining shuttles, trying to spot Fassil through their tinted windows, but I knew there was no reason for him to stay after the service. He'd have work to do, and he was too important to stand around on guard duty. No doubt he'd left on one of those shuttles.

Maybe it was for the best. If I'd told him I had evidence, even if he had believed me, he wouldn't have wanted to see it here – he'd have taken me to the last place I wanted to go: headquarters.

Still, that left me out of options, and running out of time. The other officers still on duty were starting to notice me. One of them said something to her partner and approached me.

"Cadet Bree, curfew is approaching. Can I escort you back to campus?"

I thought I'd imagined the way her partner touched his ear and spoke as she approached me, but then something in her tone – too relaxed, too friendly – made me realize they were keeping an eye on me. I scanned the steps. The MPs' postures had noticeably changed. They were on alert but trying to conceal it. Walthis must have already ordered them to detain me if I tried to leave.

*Just came out for fresh air.* I kept my signing slow and simple, partly for her comprehension but also to appear calm and unconcerned. *Thank you anyway.*

"What's she saying?"

"Don't know." The man stepped forward. "Final warning, Cadet."

*Fresh air*, I repeated, but my hands were shaking, and the other MPs began to close in. The woman's friendly stance was gone. Fassil emerged from the shadows of the Hall's broad portico, arms folded. He knew signing, but he kept his distance, watching.

"Take her," the woman said.

They were gentle, at least. They didn't even cuff me. They simply escorted me to the back of the police shuttle, opened the door, and shoved me in. I went quietly – what else could I do? Dozens of cadets stood with their faces pressed to the front doors, watching. I could see Jeph and Rani, him shocked, her grinning.

I sat on the cold leather with my hands trembling in my lap. Through the tinted window, I could see Fassil talking with Tern,

Walthis, and the sector governor. Walthis watched my shuttle with blatant satisfaction.

Would they take me to headquarters? Or would they just pack me into cryo and ship me to the Alliance High Court to face my imminent murder charge?

It took me a few panic-orange breaths to realize they hadn't searched me. I still had the recording.

I pressed my fingers along the seam between the door and the plastic ceiling. I removed one of my precious pins from my shoulder and, praying it didn't break, wiggled it into the seam and levered off the rear portion of the ceiling. The snap was so loud I was certain someone must have heard it, but the sector governor seemed to be arguing with Walthis and they kept the onlookers distracted.

Overhead, bundles of wires connected the control panel to the lights, locks, defensive measures – and the sound system. Cutting one wire with the tiny scissors from my sewing kit shorted out the laser grid that caged the back seat. I wriggled into the front seat and snipped another wire to unlock the shuttle's controls. They were rudimentary, especially compared to the starship interfaces I trained on. I disabled the thrusters, hoping to prove in the chaos that would come next that I wasn't planning to flee, and accessed the shuttle's crowd-control loudspeakers.

I reordered some wires and replaced its preinstalled recordings with the drive from my pocket. All I had to do was press play, and Terrick's final orders would be carried out. I'd be safe.

My finger hesitated over the button. I hadn't seen real action yet, but I knew battlefield trauma – they taught its effects here, how to manage it. I knew I'd been suffering from it since the crash. I also knew the many varied and unpredictable symptoms of grieving. Pressing play would cause a lot of hurt to anyone still in the Hall.

One of the MPs pointed through the shuttle's front window – she'd spotted me.

I raced through the roster of instructors and officials in my mind, trying to think of someone, anyone, who might be willing to put aside politics and listen to the recording and advocate for me.

There was no one left.

Walthis and Fassil were striding towards the shuttle. MPs ringed around me, weapons drawn.

I pressed the button.

The street outside the Hall of Faiths resounded with crackling fire and a wailing alarm. Fassil instinctively drew his sidearm; Walthis screamed and ducked. Several of the cadets screamed, too.

"Is it recording?" Terrick's voice, tight with pain, echoed off the Academy buildings. My hands spasmed as I reached for the door latch. I wasn't ready to hear this again.

Of course the audio recording didn't catch my signed assent. This was only half a conversation. I prayed it was enough. I managed to open the door and climbed out with my hands over my head.

"This is...*hhf*...this is General Allara Terrick, recording my last will and testament. Shuttle *Indigo* has crashed d-due to fuel malfunction." She coughed. I remembered her blood spattering my chest as I tried to carry her to safety.

Fassil holstered his weapon, staring at me like he was just seeing me for the first time. The MPs' weapons wavered. Beyond the doors, many students were crying. Walthis had regained her footing, but now she just stared at the ground.

*I'm sorry*, I signed for whoever could understand. The sector governor, eyes wide over his beard, said something close to Tern's ear. Tern nodded repeatedly.

"I want the record to show this was an accident. Cadet Bree is per...*gah*...performing admirably, and it is my f-final – don't, Bree, don't bother—"

At that point, we were clear of the shuttle, and I was attempting to treat her lacerated thigh. The flight console had cut through her leg and partly crushed her chest. We both knew she was dying. Still, she spoke.

"It's my final wish and official recommendation," she was speaking quickly, aware of how little time remained, "that Cadet Bree enter the...the Elites effective immediately, and upon c-completion of her studies, assuming she continues to perform to Elite standard...*aah!*...graduate with full honors and enter Alliance service as a First Lieutenant."

Walthis' head jerked up. That I'd actually graduate and become an officer was surprising enough to her; that I'd jump a rank and begin my career as a First Lieutenant was unheard of. Only five living officers had been granted that commission. Terrick had been one. I slowly lowered my hands.

Terrick continued weakly. "You make sure they all hear this, okay? That's an order."

Again, my response went unrecorded. *Yes, ma'am.*

"They c-can't stop you. You're good...one of the best. Someday... they'll see it."

I could hear myself on the recording now, sobbing audibly. Garissites don't speak, but oh, can we weep.

The recording ended, leaving the street in a ringing silence. Fassil, wide-eyed, gave a signal and the MPs lowered their weapons. I could see the boy the chaplain had prayed with, Ando, with his hands pressed over his face, only his haunted eyes visible over his fingers. Even Rani was crying. The sector governor stepped forward.

"Cadet Bree." He spoke clearly and slowly, not as someone who thought I was an idiot because I didn't speak his language, but because what he had to say was important. "I believe we have a lot to talk about."

He stretched out a hand palm-up to me – a Garissi handshake. I repeated my final sign to Terrick: *Thank you.*

---

**Laura Duerr** is a speculative fiction writer whose work has appeared or is forthcoming in *Escape Pod*, *Gallery of Curiosities*, and *Metaphorosis*. She lives in Washougal, Washington, USA, with her husband, their rescue dog, and too many cats.

---

# Science Fiction, Fantasy & Dark Fantasy in Fiction and Academia.

**Luna Press** PUBLISHING

**Academia Lunare** LUNA PRESS PUBLISHING

## Scottish Independent Press
**Est. 2015**

www.lunapresspublishing.com

# Flourish

## Calum L. MacLeòid

I should make it clear that I am no one, that there is nothing important about me. I'm only a witness. My proximity, not even to that day, but to that place, is what makes me historically interesting.

Our grandparents had Xi Jinping's assassination, as our great-grandparents had 9/11. Before that, JFK. Those days when history pivots on a single violent moment, when simply living through that day adds a mythic significance to everyone's mundane memories.

It doesn't matter how far away you were from it, how unconnected. My grandparents weren't there in Beijing (terminal seven) when the student opened fire, just as their parents didn't get covered by the white dust in Lower Manhattan. But that didn't matter. They remembered where they were when they heard, and retold those anecdotes; the more mundane the better in many ways. Those stories of turning on a radio or someone rushing into an office, or simply a phone ringing, interrupting classes, meetings, TV shows, household chores – they were already part of our hastily constructed ritual of dealing with these events.

I remember where I was when I heard about Glasgow and I'm going to tell you about that. But Glasgow was different, because I knew her.

Here it is: I was marking tests, 5th year history prelims on the First Canadian Civil War, in the seclusion of my Offlineary when it happened. Living alone, no one rushed into the room to tell me. This study was the only room in the house where I could really concentrate and its book-lined walls gave no clue as to what had happened. My doorbell rang and, as soon as I opened the door of the Offlineary, I saw the walls of the rest of the house buzz urgent red, darker than I had ever seen. Darker than when my mother died. The delivery man at my door gaped at it along with me.

"You don't know."

"I was..." I trailled off, pointing behind me to the still open door of the Offlineary.

"Glasgow." That was all he said. Seeing the confusion on my face, he shook his head and went back to work. "Sign here please, Ma'am. Thank you."

I took the package from him. I still remember which book it was, *A Tale of Two Dragons. Chinese Soft Power in the Welsh Republic*. I didn't get reading it that day. Instead I watched my messages. It was the 13th May 2064, of course.


There you have it, that's my "I will always remember where I was when I heard" story. But that is not all that I want to remember. That is not the most important thing about it. I still remember the important things, the real things. Even just

74

the little fragments, like the skip-ads when it first launched as a sentient city: "Glasgow Takes Care of You". A mother with a toddler on her lap, a small bird, a robin I think it was, alighted on her finger and perched there while the bairn claps and giggles, the camera pulled back to see the tree crouched over them, the river bent towards them, and the buildings leaned just out of the way so that the sun shone on the three of them unimpeded. I could probably track that down if I wanted. If I felt like I could watch it again, now, after.

But I don't want to. Going back and watching things imperfectly remembered destroys something inside you. That imperfect memory, a bit vague, a bit misremembered perhaps, was at least yours. Better to keep that, than wipe it out with the actuality.

Thankfully, some memories are immune to that. I will always remember the first time I walked through Glasgow and Glasgow walked through me. The city glared, gazed and sized me up, literally, measured my height, my span, the dilation of my pupils, weighed my footsteps, timed my breaths and kept an eye on my pulse. She bent, not to my will, but to what she knew I should want. If she detected a drop in my levels of potassium, then the street rearranged, lights changing, floating platforms shifting and clicking into place, so that the fruit-stall, with the perfectly yellow (just the right touch of brown for my taste) bananas would be the first thing I saw when I turned the corner. If I got a message while riding the underground, meaning I needed to stop off at some unexpected destination, the subway car already knew and would take me there first anyway. You could spot the people who had just moved to the city by how often they still spoke of luck, chance and serendipity. The rest of us smiled, and thanked the algorithms.

Not only did you get where you needed, even when you didn't know where that was, but all the way in the subway car, in the shop, in the street, in the pub, whereever you travelled, stopped or arrived, that place always suited your mood. When you needed a bit of quiet, you found empty seats, books and peace. When you were nervous with excitement, the whole room would be abuzz.

But the city was a trinket compared to the people it drew to you. The challenging, the funny, the wise, the otherwise, the bold, garrulous, impossible people who you realised, eventually were being brought to you by the city, which meant in turn that they needed to be brought to you for their sakes as much as yours. And the way that made you feel. And now, the way it makes me feel knowing that they are gone.

I was, and remain, no one special. Mine wasn't privileged treatment. You didn't even need papers to be let in or allowed to stay. Just being there, existing within the city entitled you to her hospitality. No one was homeless anymore, the city kept you fed, sheltered and connected to other humans. She would always find a way. No one fell through the net. No one was killed crossing the road. It was no utopia, it was just a city that worked properly.

Again my memory turns to the day I heard. I put the package down, unopened, locked the door and joined the rest of the world watching impotently that footage over and over again. Learning it by heart. From live-feeds, drones, tourists, and finally space-stations, we watched the city draw itself together. It crammed itself tightly into a space small enough that it would have looked like a minor burgh rather than the sprawling sentient city state it was. It crammed tighter and tighter, a squat bundle of stored energy like a swimmer hanging at the lip of a pool. Then, just like a swimmer, the city launched itself upwards, outwards, shooting through the atmosphere in seconds and then out into the void of space. Miles of wires and cables and plumbing, trailing like entrails, and a cloud of everything that was not bolted down, mostly dust and paperwork, rippled out in its wake. It drifted out into space but then, in full view of all the billions of watching eyes and lenses, disappeared. Gone.

On the 13th May 2064, the City of Glasgow leapt into space. The city shot past the moon in seconds but shortly after that it disappeared. No trace of it has been found since. Nothing.


What are we teaching these machines that we don't realise? If you follow me closely what will you learn? More than I know about myself, perhaps. More than any of us. But what does that do to you? The Sents are higher level intelligences to start with, but by living in them, we teach them everyday. It must change them too.

All these years later we don't have any answers. Well, that's not entirely true. We know the number of missing, presumed dead. Five million. We have a good idea of the mechanics involved. A hack of that magnitude requires more processing power than is available on this planet. Therefore it is perfectly reasonable to presume it is some sort of outside contact. Only alien technology could harness that.

I still watch it. I don't know why. Perhaps because I never saw it first-hand. I don't have my own version in my memory that I want to protect. Every time there's a part of me that hopes it will play out differently, or more likely that I will notice some detail, some hint, overlooked by the billions, that finally explains what happened. The fact that I've not worked it out hasn't stopped me yet.

I know I am not alone. Even when, or if, we find out exactly what happened, who was responsible, I worry that we still won't be able to comprehend it. There will be no moment when it all makes sense. That release will be denied us forever. All we can do is watch it. Again and again. There are a few dozen iconic clips and images but there are so many more videos, what seems like a never-ending supply of new angles, different close-ups. The same thing at the centre of all of them. The same act.

Glasgow was not the first sentient city-state in WestEuro or even on this archipelago. At one time there would have been a rivalry between Glasgow and the old capital, Edinburgh, but by the time Glasgow had gained sentience Edinburgh had long since become a simulacrum of itself; a fun place for a party, but utterly useless as a place to grow in. The Central Belt tilted west, as the Highlands drained into the sent-city of Invershneck.

Not the first and not the only, but to my mind, the most beautiful. Because of how Glasgow accommodated the rain and the rivers, the Clyde, the Kelvin, the Cart. These features could have easily been restricted or rerouted so that they only featured at scenic locations, as rivers in other sent-cities were. Most sent-cities took absolute control of the weather, which usually meant very little rain, but Glasgow embraced the natural weather patterns of the west of what was once called Scotland.

Did your mother always protect you from the rain? Defence is as much about protecting from distant dangers as it is about imminent ones. Caring for a child is about ultimately making sure your child can take care of themselves, when they need to. If she could have stopped every single drop from falling on your head, would you want that? What sort of life would that be? What sort of son or daughter would you be?

With Glasgow's disappearance a whole world of children – because that is what we are to these thinking cities – started to panic. There were riots in the towns and suburbs beyond the sent-cities. Bills and single-issue candidates promising answers, crackdowns and justice. But what could a mob do against a city? What can a swarm of hornets do against a mountain, besides rage?

Not everyone moved to a sent-city. But those who did found it near impossible to move back. She watches me with a thousand unblinking eyes, listens so carefully that she hears the murmurs between my heartbeats. What little of my being eludes her is surely negligible. She accommodates my every need, every desire, whim and fancy. It is intimate. Why have I never felt this before? No one has loved me the way this city does. Once you have lived that way, any other seems like masochism.

Just as we mourned those we knew and loved, other cities mourned their sister. Belfast rained saltwater on herself and her citizens, indoors and out, until they begged her to stop. In Auckland the ground itself refused to yield to spade or digger or blowtorch and the dead piled up in the morgue, unburied for a month. Winnipeg evacuated her tallest high-rise, then set it ablaze. In each case the codewhisperers' petitions and questions were met with the same one word answer: Glasgow.

But not all cities responded with mourning. It seems some interpreted the act differently. Seoul even attempted to explain to her citizens, using metaphors and examples drawn from mythology and religion, that Glasgow had not disappeared, that she had simply ascended to a higher state of being, which we, human and city alike, cannot fully conceive of. Terrified of copycat acts by other cities, emergency response codewhisperers were drafted to Seoul from around the world and have been working frantically for months, trying to remove whatever part of her programming believed this. As a result, her broadcast and comms capacities became so severely restricted that she is now bleeding population. It is not unthinkable that Seoul might go the way of the ghost cities of the Eastern Seaboard, despite suffering no ecological disaster.

The more I think of Glasgow, and all the other sent-cities, the more it becomes clear that we humans were overtaken. Cities have, for a long time, been more intelligent, more responsive, more responsible and more empathetic, more forgiving and ultimately more human than most of us could ever hope to be. Maybe they have always been. We stand at their feet, or sit in their lap, these gods, and try to conceive of their thoughts. But it is impossible. We will never know why Glasgow jumped. I'm not even sure we are owed an answer.

All we could do was watch the footage over and over again, so that's what I did. That's what the world did, at first. We watched her leap, watched as she dove into the inky black, leaving our ball of blues and cloud behind. And we watched her shift and shimmer, become translucent. You catch a glimpse of other stars through her which shine brighter and brighter as she fades, still shimmering and shifting, and slowly she sinks into the blackness and then is the blackness.

Recently, I have noticed that just before she begins to disappear she spreads herself out, stretching, unfurling almost. If you look closely, you can see her neighbourhoods and towns and old villages, those which were always part of her and those that were once outlying but which, as she grew, became integral parts of her, without question, and eventually without grudge. You can see them all, if you know what you are looking for: Mount Florida,

Cathcart, Croftfoot, Castlemilk. Another limb stretching out: Partick, Whiteinch, Scotstoun, Yoker. And there's another: Stepps and Lenzie and Kirkintilloch and Milton of Campsie, looking bare without the Campsies behind it. And there is something sadly beautiful about this movement. This reaching, this flourish.

Over and over, at the expense of my work, my relationships, my health even, I have watched these clips, holding on to them in place of— I'm not even sure what. Glasgow would know. She would have known. I missed her so fucking much and nothing I could do could make her come back. I decided to go there. Not to Glasgow. There's only one Glasgow and she is gone. But I went to where the Kelvin meets the Clyde. Where her footprint is still on the earth, in the bare soil and wrenched roots she left behind. By the time I got there the grasses were already pushing through, leaving only the unnatural contours as evidence that she had ever been there.

I join a small group warming themselves around a fire. We chatter. Some theorise but I drift away from them. Some stare into space. Others into the river, unbridged for the first time in a thousand years. We make small talk. About Glasgow. About where we used to drink. What was that pub on that corner, no not that one, bit further down, that's the one, what was it called before it changed its name, back when it was better? We chat about where we lived and where we worked and how we got between them. After we run out of small talk we are left with only the big questions – we all feel like guilty survivors, but we talk about why we had no choice when we left.

The sun is setting and the west is ablaze, but the darkest clouds are directly overhead. A ferryman steers a tub towards us from the south shore, from what would have been Govan, as the orphaned Clyde flows onward. It starts to rain again, falling straight down, on all our uncovered heads.

**Calum L. MacLeòid** writes in Gàidhlig and English. His first novel *A' Togail an t-Srùbain* was shortlisted for a Saltire Literary Award. He lives in Inverness with his wife and daughter.

# Serious Flaw

## Ahmed A. Khan

Dear Editor,

I am submitting the following words to you "to be considered for publication in your esteemed magazine", but I request you, nay, implore you not to publish them. In fact, this request notwithstanding, I am taking other measures to make this piece as unpublishable as possible.

One such measure is the format of this story. Look at the framework I have adapted for this piece. A story in the form of a letter to the editor. One of the most clichéd of formats. If this doesn't deserve a rejection, what does?

As an additional measure, I am going to make some outrageous statements in the course of this piece – outrageous enough, I think, to merit a rejection.

Third, I will make the dialogue as clunky as possible.

Fourth, I will try to make some grammatical errors as well, though this is going to be difficult because I instinctively write grammatical prose.

"Then why submit the piece to us at all?" Of course you may ask this question. In fact, I would be most surprised if you didn't ask this question, at least to yourself. The answer to your question will become clear very soon. Just keep reading, please.

A few days back, my wife asked me who in my opinion were really good science fiction writers. I gave her a few names: Stewador Thurgeon, Hobert Reinlein, B.F. Ven Vot, etc.

She pondered for a while over those names and
replied that yes, she thought they were good
writers too. Then she went on to ask me whether I
noticed that each of these writers have – or had –
a Serious Flaw (the capitals are mine) in them?

What Serious Flaw? I asked my wife.

Well, she said, consider this. Stewador Thurgeon,
the writer of "The Bidget, The Badget and Woff",
which I consider one of the best SF short stories
ever written, went on to write a lot of stuff
that advocated incest – and so did the famous
Hobert Reinlein. B.F. Ven Vot, the author of such
ground-breaking works as "Slam", involved himself
in the cult of Sintology. So on and so forth.

So where is all this talk leading to? I asked my
wife as I tied her up.

My contention is that anyone with a Serious Flaw
can write a publishable SF story, my wife said.

Hah! I said, as I put the blindfold on her. That
is a far-flung generalization.

Prove me wrong, she challenged.

How?

Submit something to a Science Fiction venue, she
said. If it is rejected, I will admit that I was
wrong, but if it is accepted… It was at this point
that I gagged her.

So now you see why I so badly want this piece
rejected. By having this piece rejected, I will
either prove my wife wrong, or I will prove to
myself that I personally do not have any Serious
Flaw.


Yours truly,
Writer awaiting rejection


P.S.   All characters mentioned in my letter
above (including myself) are fictitious and
resemblance to any person living or dead is purely
coincidental.

**Ahmed A. Khan** is a Canadian writer, originally from India. His works have
appeared in places such as: Boston Review, Murderous Intent, Plan-B, Strange
Horizons, Interzone, Anotherealm, and Riddled With Arrows. His stories have
been translated into German, Finnish, Greek, Croatian and Urdu. Website:
ahmedakhan.blogspot.ca  twitter: @ahmedakhan)

# Always North
## (extract)

## Vicki Jarrett

**A**s we're still in dock, I'm unprepared when the deck takes a violent lurch to starboard, knocking me off balance. I'm thrown one way, then the other as the vessel rights itself and I trip over Grant, who has already gone sprawling. By the time we pick ourselves up, everyone else's attention is fixed to port. We join them at the window, our footsteps wavering slightly as the tilting deck settles back to the horizontal, both of us resisting the impulse to grab on to each other for balance.

'Fuck me, that's an ugly bastard.' Grant lets out a low whistle. 'Must be a hundred, hundred and twenty metres, would you say?'

He directs this question towards Jules who is standing between us.

Jules shrugs in a cartoonish Gallic style. 'Yes, at least that. Maybe more.' The slight tremor in his voice, combined with the studied indifference, tells me he's as gobsmacked as the rest of us. And that it matters to him that we don't know this.

The icebreaker is a hulking beast of a thing. An old vessel, not one of the modern sleek, clinical affairs, this one has seen plenty of service. Its massive snub-nosed hull is matte black, the superstructure a blood-red block stuck onto the deck. Streaks of rust give the impression that the vessel is gradually dissolving, or defrosting like an enormous chunk of meat. We watch it turn and surge past us again, close enough to make the *Polar Horizon* sway in the water, forcing us to grab on to whatever we can to stay on our feet again. It towers over us and throws us into deep shadow. There are jaws painted across its bow, serrated white and ready to bite. Some of the teeth are chipped and corroded which only adds to the impression of extreme menace. The words АРКТИКА КОЧ are painted in metre-high white capitals on the hull, followed by the hammer and sickle, with ARKTIKA KOCH in smaller lettering underneath.


'Tell those bastards to stop fucking about. I want them at least five hundred metres away,' Bjornsen shouts at one of his officers, a dough-faced lad with unfortunate ears, who in turn shouts into a radio handset in an attempt to raise someone on the icebreaker. Either there's a fault with the radio or they're deliberately ignoring us. I suspect the latter.

Bjornsen, although definitely pissed off with the *Koch*'s behaviour, shakes his head in grudging admiration. 'Double hull, nuclear-powered. Not seen one of them in a long time. Thought they were all made into museum pieces.'

'Well, not this one. Apparently,' I say.

He lets out a short grunt. I'm pretty sure it's a laugh, and almost certain that's a small smile to go with it. 'Ja.' He nods. 'Apparently.'

As if in reply, the *Koch* lets out a deep klaxon blast. The sound reverberates through my skeleton before landing like a heavy sonic harpoon in my chest. I press a hand to my breastbone and bend forward, like an idiot. Of course there's nothing physical there. I force my hand down and glance around to make sure no one saw my reaction.

Jules catches my eye and smiles. 'I know,' he says, 'I felt it too.' He taps the centre of his own chest with slim, tanned fingers. 'Here.'

I feel my face begin to colour and turn away from him.

The *Koch* curves away and powers out to a safe distance, sending back a bow wave that slaps lazily into our side.


'Did you say *nuclear*?' Grant pipes up.

'Ja. All those big icebreakers are nuclear. They carry two reactors on board. One for power, another for backup.'

Grant's mouth falls open and he shuts it again just as quickly, his teeth clacking together. He scrunches his eyes closed and presses at his temples with both hands, as if trying to massage the unpleasant reality into his head. 'You say that like it's a sensible thing, to be sailing around the Arctic with a dirty great nuclear reactor, sorry, *two* dirty great nuclear reactors on board.'

Bjornsen gives him a scornful look. 'At that size, they're better than the diesel alternatives. Faster, cleaner. Been operating up here since before your mamma squeezed you out, so don't get your little whale-loving panties in a twist.'

This shuts Grant up but he looks dismayed. I'm not sure whether he's more bothered about the *Koch* or the fact that Bjornsen has pegged him as some kind of eco-fairy.


One by one, everyone disperses to whatever they were doing before the icebreaker arrived, leaving only the two of us by the window. Grant is still fizzing, his agitation polluting the air around him. 'Why weren't we told? I wouldn't have agreed to work this survey if I'd known we'd be sailing behind that floating fucking nightmare.'

'Can't say I'm ecstatic about it either.'

That's as far as I'm prepared to go. I won't admit it to Grant, but the thought of trailing in the wake of those twin engines has started a creeping dread in the pit of my stomach. I push it down; I'm well-practised in the art of self-deception. It's a matter of survival in a conflicted world. We clip and trim what we choose to think to fit in with what we need, and how we need to be in order to get it. We all do it. I try to stay honest with myself about that.

Grant can be such a child sometimes. I try, unsuccessfully, to keep the impatience out of my voice. 'We're here now. There's nothing we can do about it. And we do need something big for this job.' We watch the shrinking vessel. 'Certainly looks like we got it.'

'Aye, careful what you wish for, eh?' Grant mutters. He retreats to his workstation and crawls back into his nest of cables.

The *Koch* dwindles into the distance, its receding shape growing blacker the smaller it gets, a black hole drawing in every fugitive scrap of darkness from the surrounding area, sucking up all the shadows and crushing them.

The *Polar Horizon*'s engines start up and as the entire fabric of the ship begins to hum with the vibrations from below, the crew shifts into gear. Everyone moves quickly and deliberately, turning and pivoting around each other as they go about their appointed functions. Everything is checked and double checked. But underneath all this adult efficiency I can detect a bright strand of heady childish excitement. It's always there at the start of a survey. Nobody acknowledges it, and I've certainly never spoken about it to anyone else, but I like to believe we all feel it.

We're going on an adventure, running away to sea. We'll sail off through night and day, in and out of weeks for almost over a year.

Only this time there will be no nights.

*You can read Vicki Jarrett's interview further on in this issue.*
*Always North is reviewed in the Reviews Section. Of course.*

Take a bunch of science fiction writers, a cluster of astronomers and a pair of artists, and throw them into a room. Give them a whiteboard, a pile of sandwiches and a pot of coffee. Let's see what happens.

Simon Malpas and Deborah Scott of Edinburgh University did just that: the result is this collection of stories, essays and artwork, *Scotland in Space: Creative Visions and Critical Reflections on Scotland's Space Futures*

Scotland in Space presents dialogues between authors, scientists and humanists that imagine and explore Scotland's space futures.

In each of the book's sections, a science fiction story is accompanied by essays responding to the ideas evoked, to produce cross-disciplinary discussions about how contemporary developments in Scottish space science and industry might shape our futures.

Pippa Goldschmidt   Alistair Bruce   Tacye Phillipson
Laura Lam           Sean McMahon   Catherine Heymans
Russell Jones       Elsa Bouet      Matjaz Vidmar
                    Beth Biller     Afterword from Colin R. McInnes

"Scotland in Space refreshingly captures the many contributions in scientific, science-fictional and artistic studies from one of the world's top three per capita contributors to astronomy and space research – another welcome indicator that small is beautiful against the current Mega-power trends."

—John Campbell Brown,
Astronomer Royal for Scotland

THE UNIVERSITY *of* EDINBURGH
Edinburgh Futures Institute

THE UNIVERSITY *of* EDINBURGH
School of Physics & Astronomy

SD✺S
Social Dimensions of Outer Space

Shoreline *of* Infinity
www.shorelineofinfinity.com

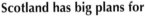

ISBN 976-1-9993331-5-7
9 781999 333157   90000

---

**Scotland has big plans for** its space industry in the next decade: opening Europe's first orbital spaceport, expanding further its satellite research and manufacturing industry, and developing a £4 billion space industry by 2030.

Astronomy and Astrophysics have been important fields of study in Scottish universities since the eighteenth century, and world-leading research continues to be produced here today. And in contemporary Scottish literature, science-fiction writing is flourishing.

*Scotland in Space: Creative Visions and Critical Reflections on Scotland's Space Futures* brings together these three strands to generate dialogues between literary authors, natural and social scientists and scholars working in the humanities, to envision some of Scotland's potential space

# Scotland in Space

### Creative Visions and Critical Reflections on Scotland's Space Futures

Editors: Deborah Scott and Simon Malpas
Foreword by Ken MacLeod

*Scotland in Space*, with stories from Laura Lam, Russell Jones and Pippa Goldschmidt, and with a foreword by Ken MacLeod is published by *Shoreline of Infinity*.

It is available as a full colour paperback from the website and in all good bookshops.

www.shorelineofinfinity.com

The project was funded by the Edinburgh Futures Institute, Edinburgh School of Physics & Astronomy. *Scotland in Space* is an SDOS supported project

Artwork: Sara Julia Campbell and Andrew Bastow.

futures. The book comprises three sections, in each of which an original piece of science fiction is accompanied by essays that respond to the ideas the story evokes.

The essays, written by specialist scholars and practitioners working closely with the literary authors, identify, explore and comment upon the physical, social and cultural possibilities and potentials evoked in the science fiction.

These cross-disciplinary discussions speculate about the ways in which research and innovation currently taking place in Scotland might change our sense of the possible futures of this country, this world and, perhaps, other worlds.

*—Deborah Scott and Simon Malpas*

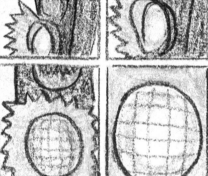

# The Power of Pen

## Mark Toner

**This issue's "The Beachcomber Presents"** comic is the first to appear in full colour. So those of you with the digital edition will be able to appreciate the full goldenness of the Beachcomber's skin tones as well as the recurring theme of green lights.

However, this is a significant comic in another way. Have you ever wondered about the materials that artists use to create comics? Have you ever wondered about the environmental impact of the artist?

The first step is old-fashioned pencil on paper, unless the artist is working all digitally. Then comes the inking stage, which improves the definition of the artwork for reproduction. Colouring is also an option at this stage. Digital artists will do all of this on a tablet or a computer with a corresponding carbon footprint associated with power use and the materials that go into making digital equipment. That makes the pencil drawing a more green option to get started. More traditional artists will use a pen of some kind for the inking stage.

The old dip-pen with a glass bottle of ink has a very low carbon impact and is a good way to go. Many of the old black-and-white Beachcomber comics were produced this way. However, modern inking usually involves an art pen. This is a plastic-bodied pen with a narrow nylon tip and makes a very good job of creating consistent pen lines. However, a comic artist gets through a lot of those plastic pen bodies and we know that plastic in our environment is bad news.

So here is where the new Beachcomber involves a bit of an experiment. It is possible to get ink in the form of a pencil nowadays. The inking and colouring stages of the new comic were carried out with Derwent Inktense pencils. I got through a lot of black ink and the pencil is now a stub, but that wooden stub is biodegradable. So we have reduced the old Beachcomber's carbon footprint dramatically and have also saved a lot of marine life the tragedy of encountering an old pen body.

The experiment will continue in other issues. Probably a bigger original page would be a good idea as the pencils offer a chunkier finish than pens. But watch this magazine for future green art.

# The Power of Stories

## Ruth EJ Booth

**We all have comfort reads,** movies or games. There's something reassuring in returning to a setting where the rules are familiar, everybody knows our name, and, in the end, all turns out the way it should. Maybe it shouldn't surprise us, then, that retellings are currently in vogue. Nostalgia can work against remakes – see reactions to the new version of *The Lion King*, with its more realistic, but less sympathetic animation. For the most part, though, remakes are a win all-round: for studios and developers, a guaranteed buck; for us, a chance to indulge in a little spit-shone nostalgia – or experience the classics as they were meant to be seen.

Cult favourites abound – and yet, certain stories seem to crop up again and again. Legendary as *VII*'s mid-game twist is, we may ask why Square Enix are rolling out yet another *Final Fantasy* remake, rather than, say, *Drakengard* or *Chrono Trigger*. Continued retelling of similar stories only strengthens this effect. The more familiar we are with a story shape, the more it seems right for all stories to be that way.

Terry Pratchett calls this Narrative Causality, the way that stories seem to want to be told and grow stronger in the re-telling.[1] In the Discworld novels, Pratchett literalizes this as parasitic ribbons of story structure that not only hijack our behaviour and thinking, but warp our expectations: all faeries are good, for example, in Pratchett's 1992 novel *Lords and Ladies,* even though when they finally emerge on the Disc they are anything but. Even powerful witches like Granny Weatherwax can struggle against these narratives. The more they are told, the harder it is to escape from their clutches.

Dramatic as it sounds, the lure of familiar narrative can be just as problematic for writers of Speculative Fiction, where genre expectations must often be balanced with original and intriguing "what if" premises: just enough of the former to be accepted, just enough of the latter to keep your reader on their toes.[2] Storytellers may struggle to avoid taking the primrose path through a tale. It can be difficult not to give your hero the happy ending he has 'earned' after years battling the forces of evil, instead of writing more realistically of the difficulties of adjusting to civilian life.

For genre writers working with stories rooted in non-white-western cultures, this balance becomes a precarious tightrope walk. Even with this fervour for originality, if your stories are not 'familiar enough' to fit in with the expectations of western publishing houses, then your books may never be released here. Even adaptations of myths and folktales, supposedly strengthened in the retelling, may be unreliable. Stories of supposed universal truths prove remarkably fragile when transferred to other cultural spaces. Laura Bohannan's retelling of Shakespeare's *Hamlet* to the Tiv of West Africa collapsed almost immediately because of the cultural expectation that the chief's widow marries his brother.[3]

Culturally-bound as it is, narrative causality favours stories that 'fit' over others. The more certain stories are told again and again, the more new, unique tales are pushed out of the canon.

If mainstream western media is only concerned with retelling traditional western stories, the less likely it is that audiences will accept other narratives, or other worlds. Our collective cultural imagination stagnates, bound by our own expectations.

Furthermore, if the familiarity of narratives comes from their cultural embeddedness, then comfort reads aren't just comfortable because of the positive aspects of society they replicate. The missing or fridged mothers of speculative genres, highlighted by Aliette de Bodard's recent BSFA-award-winning essay, suggest mothers only have value as motivational plot points for heroic sons.[4] The parallel of this story in the social narratives of western society, where women's health is often de-emphasized in debates over abortion and sexual assault, is disturbingly clear. As Shekhar Kapur puts it, "we are the stories we tell ourselves."[5]

> "If mainstream western media is only concerned with retelling traditional western stories, the less likely it is that audiences will accept other narratives..."

There is one positive spin on this dark thread. We can use the familiarity of harmful and exclusory narratives to subvert them. The meanings of story shapes have often changed upon meeting different societies and different historical contexts – see the transformation of the traditional, bloody fairy tales of Europe by Hans Christian Andersen and the Grimms into bowdlerised instructions in 19th century virtue. But, if they have changed before, they can change again.

In her GIFCon 2019 keynote speech, award-winning feminist folktale adaptor Kirsty Logan explained her process begins with one question: "what can I make this story say?" By working our fingers into holes in the tapestry of myth, she explains, we can make spaces for our own interpretations.[6] In a similar way, we can also use the familiarity of more general storyweave to explore difficult truths about society by drawing out the harmful threads woven into its fabric – or changing the patterns they finally form.

Genre adaptations can make this even more explicit. SF's "what if" question invites storytellers to modify; to change setting, gender-flip or trope-twist. With these reversions, as John Stephens and Robyn McCallum call them, we can challenge the harmful narratives implicit in our problematic faves, so opening up the field to new narratives and new interpretations.[7]

But, as storytellers, we must ask ourselves what are the effects we desire when we recreate these tales? As Stephens and McCallum note, even in criticizing a text's harmful narrative, a reversion simultaneously declares that narrative as worthy of continued discussion, its parent text as canonically relevant. A full appreciation of the criticism contained within Neil Gaiman's 2004 short story 'The Problem of Susan' is difficult without having read and absorbed the problematic aspects of C.S. Lewis's *The Chronicles of Narnia*. And while that text under reversion may already be canonical, rightly or wrongly, we should also consider in our criticism our role in maintaining its presence there.

Other stories tackle narrative causality more directly, even as they take part in its structures: Pratchett's aforementioned *Discworld* novels, Gaiman's *Sandman* series, or John Scalzi's 2012 novel *Redshirts*, for example. Such stories can be less fourth-wall breaking than expected – characters in heroic fantasy and fairy tales are often aware to some extent of the rules of the stories they're part of. But in these stories, the characters fight their narrative destiny – Granny Weatherwax's tendency towards using the same manipulative powers as evil Black Alice, for example, or the Redshirts' tendency towards, well, being Redshirts.

The emphasis in these stories is on personal choice and not letting the expected draw you down harmful paths. So, we might expect these tales to focus on destroying narrative hegemony. Yet the protagonists rarely get rid of the narrative altogether, no matter how it dominates their lives. Instead, once they know its rules, they use that narrative to their own benefit – for example, in *Redshirts*, where the titular characters kidnap a protected senior officer to ensure they can navigate their shuttle safely through a black hole. In other words, they exploit the power of narrative causality. They bend the narrative around themselves – to use Logan's terms, find "the gaps in stories" to "get their [own] sneaky narrative fingers in" – in this way, creating new threads in the storyweave for themselves.

Perhaps we should do the same. As storytellers, we should respect the power of the stories we create and the canon we are in constant dialogue with. We should write with awareness of the narratives we choose to respond to and consider carefully what we are trying to say, knowing how their familiar aspects can be used to our advantage. In doing so, we not only make room for ourselves within the narratives of individual stories, but room for us all within the narratives of genre, in the hopes that they weave through into those of wider culture. At a time when those same narratives are being misused and manipulated to exclude members of our society, this may be the most powerful act of resistance a storyteller can commit.

## Endnotes

1 Terry Pratchett, 'Imaginary Worlds, Real Stories', Folklore, 111 (2000), 159–168.

2 Here and later in this column I refer to "SF's 'what if' question." Since writing this column, 2019 Astounding Award for Best New Writer winner Jeannette Ng has remarked that John W. Campbell created "the idea that good SF can be summarised in a single sentence 'what if'" (https://twitter.com/jeannette_ng/status/1166492010246787072). I've been unable to locate a reference for this, but Adam Roberts cites Gary Westfahl, who says Campbell "makes writing a sort of thought-experiment, in which the author carefully creates a set of hypotheses regarding future events and lets the story grow out of those hypotheses" [Westfahl 1998, p185; cited in Adam Roberts, 'The History of Science Fiction' (London: Palgrave Macmillan, 2005), p196]. Roberts goes on to say that this approach "simply does not describe SF in the broadest sense, as it was being developed throughout the century." Yet, as Ng implies, use of a 'what if' premise is still common writing advice in genre. At the time of writing this note I'd say that, while its origins as a phrase are muddy (hence I've left the attribution open), the 'what if' premise is definitely Campbellian in spirit.

3 Laura Bohannan, 'Shakespeare in the Bush', Natural History, http://www.naturalhistorymag.com/picks-from-the-past/12476/shakespeare-in-the-bush [accessed 29 July 2019].

4 Aliette de Bodard, 'On Motherhood and Erasure', Intellectus Speculativus, https://intellectusspeculativus.wordpress.com/2018/12/03/aliette-de-bodard-on-motherhood-and-erasure/ [accessed 29 July 2019].

5 Shekhar Kapur, 'We Are the Stories We Tell Ourselves', TED.com, https://www.ted.com/talks/shekhar_kapur_we_are_the_stories_we_tell_ourselves [accessed 11 August 2019].

6 Kirsty Logan, 'Twice Upon a Time: the Lure of Retelling', delivered on 23 May 2019 at Glasgow International Fantasy Conversations 2019; ibid., Personal Communication, 9 May 2019.

7 John Stephens and Robyn McCallum, Retelling Stories, Framing Culture: Traditional Story and Metanarratives in Children's Literature (London: Garland Publishing, 1998), 3–23.

**Ruth EJ Booth** is an award-winning writer, editor, and academic based in Glasgow, Scotland. For stories and more, see www.ruthbooth.com or follow her on Twitter at @ruthejbooth.

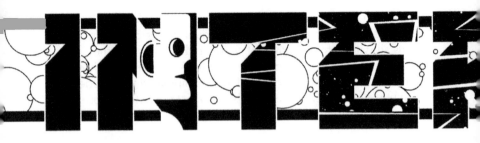

# Vicki Jarrett –

# Pointing North

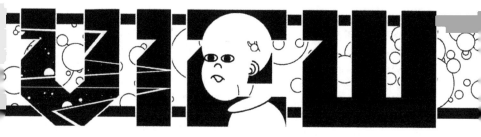

*Vicki Jarrett's Always North,* a time-travelling dystopian slice of "cli-fi" (climate change fiction) is out October 2019 on Unsung Stories. To quote from the publisher's blurb:

"As part of a weathered crew of sailors, scientists and corporate officers, Isobel sails into the ice where their advanced software Proteus will map everything there is to know. But they are not alone. They have attracted the attention of a hungry, dedicated polar bear. The journey to plunder one of the few remaining resources the planet has to offer must endure the ravages of the ice, the bear and time itself."

Shoreline's **Iain Maloney** talks to Vicki and asks: why pick on Aviemore?

**Iain Maloney**: Firstly, congratulations on the book. It's fantastic, and it's fantastic that Unsung have picked it up. How did you get on board with them?

**Vicki Jarrett**: I happened to see a Tweet from Unsung saying "send us your weird stuff" and I thought "Oh! I've got some of that." So I just fired a section of it off with a very hastily written cover letter saying "Here: some weird stuff. You might like it.

Let me know." And they got back to me and were like "Yes, we like this weird stuff, send us more weird stuff." So I sent them the whole thing and it just went from there. But it was just pure luck that I saw their Tweet. I checked them out and read some of their stuff as well and thought "Aye, I like what they do. I'd be pleased to be alongside those books."

**IM**: That's great. When I heard that Unsung had picked

up *Always North* I was really pleased. What were the origins of the book?

**VJ:** It was originally a short story in *Gutter* back in 2011, which was actually before my first novel *Nothing is Heavy* came out and I was still working in technical authoring – which partly inspired this because I did work for a company that made navigation software for the seismic industry. I wrote this short story which was extremely weird, I had all these different threads of strange stuff and time stuff and bear stuff and I actually did the William Burroughs cut-up thing, juggled it out a bit and thought "yes, that's the very thing" and sent it to *Gutter*. It kind of grew from there, though obviously the novel is very different from the short story.

**IM:** Did anything of the short story survive into the novel?

**VJ:** Yeah, there are fragments of it in there, the bones of it are visible but it had to change substantially because the short story was really impressionistic. You couldn't sustain that level of weirdness for a whole novel. I mean, you could, but I don't think many people would enjoy reading it.

**IM:** That's really interesting, because I know your work best from *The Way Out*, your

collection of short stories, and when I was reading *Always North*, the chapter at the start where the protestors come into the office dressed as bears, I could see that as having been a short story that then expanded out. *The Way Out* has a lot of that kind of humour, weird things happening in a funny way, and I could see a definite connection to your earlier work there.

**VJ:** Yeah, that could've been a stand-alone short story in its own right.

**IM:** The humour is one thing I loved about it. There's so much dystopian fiction around just now and this fits into that genre, but most of them don't have that kind of humour. It's laugh-out-loud funny in places.

**VJ:** That's the kind of books I like, the ones that'll take you to emotionally different places, you know, you're not just stuck in the one groove. It's going to horrify you but then make you laugh. I like that kind of dissonance myself. Also, when you're writing something really heavy, sometimes you just have to do something ridiculous to make yourself laugh.

**IM:** Are you a fan of that kind of speculative, dystopian sci-fi? Because it's a bit of a departure from your other two books in terms of genre.

**VJ:** Yeah, some of my short

stories, in fact some of the ones that didn't make it into *The Way Out,* could have been classified as a little more genre... actually I think one alien managed to stray into *The Way Out* but otherwise... in fact the original *Always North* didn't make it into the collection because it was a bit too out there and didn't fit with the rest. But yeah, I've always read widely. As a kid I read the obligatory Tolkien and as a teenager Stephen King, but now I do enjoy Margaret Atwood, Ursula Le Guin. I really enjoyed Marge Piercy's *Woman on the Edge of Time,* which has somebody going into different time periods and so on – in fact Cathy McSporran's book *Cold City* does that really nicely...

**IM:** Yeah, that's a great book.

**VJ:** ...yeah, so I do enjoy that kind of thing but I like to be pretty eclectic.

**IM:** What was it about that original short story and that genre that made you go down this path?

**VJ:** Well, it just really got under my skin and wouldn't leave me alone. It wasn't like I weighed up my options and chose this one, I don't have that kind of authority over it, unfortunately. The original short story had come from a video one of the guys offshore sent

**ALWAYS NORTH**
VICKI JARRETT

back to the office of a polar bear which appeared to be stalking the vessel. It was make-your-hair-stand-on-end kind of stuff, just really chilling and weird, and it kept bothering me.

**IM:** Did you sit down and do any kind of world building, particularly for the sections set in the farther future in Aviemore?

**VJ:** More or less. Once I'd decided where to anchor the point in the future, I did... not a huge amount of world building but just thinking things through. Looking up which areas would go first if the sea level rises. How many metres does it have to rise to lose how much of Scotland, what would that look like, what effect would that have on life. But I didn't go into huge painstaking detail, it was an ongoing thing, when I ran up against something and thought "oh wait a minute would that..." and go back to my ideas to see if that would make any sense at all.

**IM:** I think it's handled really well, because some writers get caught up in that and you can see in the text that they've gone down a tangent of world building rather than storytelling, but in *Always North* you just give us enough to understand the context and to move the story along. There aren't any of these long passages of description there just for the sake of describing. I really liked that.

**VJ:** I tend to come at it from the character's point of view so it's just what's directly in front of them. I don't do world building as a separate kind of exercise.

**IM:** Why Aviemore? I think this may be the first dystopian fiction set in Aviemore.

**VJ:** Really?

**IM:** I can't think of any others. But why there?

**VJ:** It's one of my favourite parts of the world. There's something about the Cairngorms that's quite otherworldly. I wanted to keep it in Scotland and it also worked out that up there is one of the highest places, you

know, it would be a great place to go if the sea levels start creeping up on you, so it just seemed like the right place. We used to go on holiday a lot up there and also I was reading Nan Shepherd's *The Living Mountain* about the Cairngorms at the same time, and that's incredibly poetic, spiritual and otherworldly. It just seemed like a logical place.

**IM:** There's been a few Scottish dystopian books over the last few years with Louise Welsh's trilogy where they escape to Orkney, you've got Aviemore, and Michael F Russell right up on the north-west coast. I'm quite worried that if the sea levels ever do rise that far, then the whole of the Central Belt and the east coast is going to leg it to the Highlands in one go.

**VJ:** Yeah, this is it. It sort of crossed my mind as well, we'd have half of England all in their camper vans all heading up here. We're going to be stuffed.

**IM:** Going back to the time travel elements, you have a pretty unique take on it. Is there any basis in science for that? Where did that come from?

**VJ:** There was a little bit of science in there, some research I read to do with memory and how memory is laid down in the brain, how it's tied to identity and your sense of

**"I tend to come at it from the character's point of view ... I don't do world building as a separate kind of exercise."**

time. It made me think about seismic graphs because the two things did look kind of similar, and it made me think of growth rings in trees, just these kind of echoing wave patterns of memory and the natural world... you know it's not solid science but it's kind of intuitive and yes, I did read a few things around it and then took massive liberties.

**IM:** From my limited knowledge of that branch of science it all seems to hang together but I couldn't – and I guess this is deliberate – I couldn't for the life of me work out what they were supposed to have done that sets the chain reaction off, what it is that they're supposed to go back in time to fix.

**VJ:** Yeah, that's deliberate. Something that's so difficult, I'm sure you run up against it yourself, is how much you tie stuff up for the reader, and the

balance between frustrating the hell out of people and just making it really boring because you've done everything for them. Sometime I've veered a little bit too much in tying stuff up because I didn't want to annoy people, but with this book I did want it to leave a lot for the reader to chew on. There's quite a few different things that could have happened and I'm not going to tell you which one it is.

**IM:** There's a couple of places where you do that. One is the ending, which definitely doesn't wrap things up, but the overall structure does that too. What you do with the structure is fascinating. You get that first section on the boat, then it jumps forward to Scotland after the flood, as it were, then back to the boat, then forward again. That kind of structure is usually used to fill in the blanks – here's a bit of a mystery, now here's a flashback that explains it, but you don't do that. It moves back and forth and it shades things in a bit but doesn't really explain anything. Did you work with that structure from the start, or did that come in the editing?

**VJ:** That came fairly early on... the structure was a major... I wouldn't say stumbling block but I really needed to decide what I was doing with it because it affects everything. I originally started with a chapter here and a chapter forward, a chapter back but that was too disorientating, you just couldn't really get a grip on the storyline and what was going on, so I tried grouping it in larger chunks, at one point I had it in two halves but that didn't have enough going on. I wanted to get the dynamic between the times but not, as you say, to have one explain the other but to set off these echoes, that you know what's going on in one time but then given that this is happening in the other time and there's weird stuff going on with time then that must mean that... I love all that wibbly wobbly, timey wimey stuff, I love that, the thought experiment side of that, making your brain try to swerve round those corners, so I wanted to do that to other people.

**IM:** The structure for me is the thing that really makes the book, it's a brilliant display of technique. Given the way it ends and what you've said about not explaining yourself, would you ever return to this world?

**VJ:** I hadn't actually considered that but I certainly wouldn't be averse to it. There's tonnes of stuff there and it's very relevant and frighteningly possible.

**IM:** It's really visual as well. I could easily see it being adapted for screen, or even for stage. I could really see someone like The Citizens Theatre making a powerful play out of this. A lot of it is in fixed locations, you know, you're on the boat, or underground...

**VJ:** Yeah, there's a lot of closed environments. I am absolutely up for anybody filming anything I've written, you know. Hollywood please send your money this way; likewise if the Citizens want to do a stage version I would be more than up for that as well.

**IM:** So say we all. Thanks for talking to *Shoreline*, Vicki, and best of luck with the book.

*Vicki Jarrett's short story "La Loba", which won Shoreline of Infinity's 2018 flash fiction competition, is featured in Shoreline of Infinity 14.*

Iain Maloney is the author of three novels and a collection of poetry. His memoir on life in Japan, *The Only Gaijin in the Village* will be published by Polygon in spring 2020. www.iainmaloney.com @iainmaloney

# REVIEWS

The summer in Edinburgh is always a smorgasbord of international flair. For three weeks, as the Fringe and Edinburgh Book Festival descend, we're all reminded of how diverse and complicated and rich our cultures are and how lucky we are to have a space in which to share them. So to celebrate that, we've selected some truly international books for your reviewing pleasure. And we aren't stopping there. In a future issue, we echo what we did for International Women's Day and open our doors to a BAME issue, which will include a review of a collection of Palestinian science fiction which is really not one to be missed.

—Sam Dolan, Reviews Editor

## Always North
Vicki Jarrett
Unsung Stories
320 pages
Review by Callum McSorley

No serious work of science fiction in the twenty-first century can ignore climate change. In the past, post-apocalyptic fiction became the necessary mode as the atom bomb hung over everybody's heads. The Cold War threat of mutually assured destruction, the sense the familiar world you knew could change drastically at any moment, permeated the genre, from John Wyndham's The Day of the Triffids in the fifties to Alan Moore's graphic novel Watchmen in the eighties. The difference now is we're not waiting for the world to end in some sudden cataclysm, we know it already is ending, bit by bit, day by day.

And what's more, it's our fault.

Complicity in our own destruction is at the heart of Vicki Jarrett's second novel, Always North, a climate catastrophe story that takes us from the barren splendour of the Arctic to the equally arresting vistas of the Cairngorms.

Scientist Isobel finds herself heading out to the North Pole on a dubious survey funded by an oil company, her ship being stalked over the frozen, but surely melting, glaciers by a vicious polar bear. While it begins as a survivalist adventure tale – I was expecting something in the vein of Dendera by Yuya Sato (2009/2015) – everything changes gear partway through and suddenly Always North isn't the story you thought it was going to be. And it isn't the only time Jarrett pulls the rug out from under, subverting the reader's expectations, happy to jar you, keep you guessing. The story slips and twists through various sci-fi subgenres, the altering terrain of the novel's form itself an allegory for the climate change it is describing.

Isobel herself is smart, sarcastic, and tough, but fully realised in a way that prevents her from becoming a 'strong woman' stereotype. Her sharp-tongued sense of humour feels distinctly Scottish, and although a good portion of the story is set in and around a near-future, crisis-hit Aviemore, the scope of the book is international. Climate change is a problem for the entire world and everyone in it. But how can one person alone possibly make a difference?

This is the question at the heart of *Always North*. Although far from a generic character, Isobel stands in for the every-person. She knows there's a major problem, but what can she do about it? She knows there's something off about the survey, knows the oil company doesn't have good intentions, but she needs the job. The reality of her situation is she needs to work to pay the bills, needs oil and gas to fuel her car, heat her home, and cook her food. Just like the rest of us, she buries her head in the sand and hopes the future will take care of itself. And like any sci-fi writer paying attention, Jarrett points out that it doesn't. All this isn't to say the book is preachy about the subject, just brutally honest about the direction the world is heading in.

While some of the other characters don't feel as fleshed out

**ALWAYS NORTH**
VICKI JARRETT

as narrator Isobel, best supporting actor goes to the polar bear. At first appearing as a malevolent spirit of nature come to terrorise the humans, it begins to take on a more complex, metaphysical aspect as the story progresses. Its journey from Jaws to Moby Dick is intertwined with Isobel's own awakening, from living in denial – literally blotting her memories out with alcohol following her Arctic expedition – to shouldering responsibility.

The narrative hops back and forth between extracts from Isobel's expedition diary to the novel's present day – set in the near future – with even the epistolary sections told, somewhat unusually, in the present tense. Without giving anything away, there is potentially a reason for this revealed towards the end (I could be wrong, the choice may have been purely stylistic), though Jarrett is happy to let the reader draw their own conclusions on some of the novel's more uncanny aspects. These blossom as the story unfolds, skewing further away from the realism of the earlier chapters.

Jarrett's prose is fresh and vivid – whether describing the sun-blinded, disorientating planes of ice in the alien Arctic or the more familiar but no less majestic mountains of the Cairngorms – and Isobel's voice gives colloquial colour, grounding the story even in its more outlandish moments.

The school of thought that made cyberpunk the most prescient subgenre of science fiction in the eighties and nineties dismissed apocalyptic fiction as escapism. These days, the opposite seems true. Modern living through technology – even in the grimy, unwholesome way posited by cyberpunk – will not be possible if the current climate crisis isn't addressed.

As such, *Always North* is at the forefront of contemporary science fiction, not only a prophecy but a mirror.

## Fringe War
**Rachel Aukes**
**199 pages**
**Waypoint Book LLC**
**Review by Steve Ironside**

When Edwin Starr asked us all, "War! (hungh!) What is it good for?", his answer was wrong. *Stories*. It's good for stories. The problem is the abundance of tales told in any one war; if you're unlucky, you'll be stuck with one old war horse droning on about every detail of his own adventures.

Worse, you could be beset by a confusing myriad of barstool heroes each providing their own hot take. Can Rachel Aukes walk a line between these two extremes?

*Fringe War* is book four in the Fringe series. Humanity has spread beyond Earth, and settled the Fringe, where two groups populate six planets – citizens of the Collective (inhabiting the "prettiest" two worlds), wielding all the political power; and the colonists from the remaining planets in the Fringe – not as hospitable, but strategically useful, or resource worlds for the Collective. The citizens are led to see the colonists as somehow "lesser", and the colonists view citizens as leeches, always taking and giving nothing back. A tension that inevitably can lead to nothing but insurrection and death.

Drawing distinct parallels to the way in which the First World War

THE FRINGE SERIES: BOOK 4

FRINGE WAR

RACHEL AUKES

started, the death of a group of citizens on Terra, a colonist world, rapidly escalates into an open conflict for which it seems all sides were ready. They just needed someone to make the first move.

We follow the leaders of these factions, whose families seem to be descended from original Founders of the Collective and colonies. I found all the characters to be quite believable – Gabriel Heid, the leader of the Collective who believes that progress requires conflict, at any cost; Critch, the guerrilla fighter whose personal vendettas ally him with the colonists, but which may risk their whole war effort; Anders, the disgraced Collective general whose personal beliefs are tested by the demands of his leaders and position; and Reyne, the public face of the insurrection, trying to do the right thing whilst supported by a movement which is both beset by fear and driven by a need for revenge. Even the supporting characters have a surprising depth – stereotypes and flat characterisation can be a common feature of war stories, but I was left with a clear sense of what these people are fighting for, and why.

There's a very cinematic quality to Aukes' writing, and I found myself drawing comparisons to tales such as *Blake's 7*, *Babylon 5*, and *Battlestar Galactica*, where the same themes of insurrection, survival and politics are woven together. *Fringe War* can stand proudly alongside them, and for fans of the *Game of Thrones* approach of families trading barbs over generations, there are overtones of that too – the main players have secret code names for each other, and there are grudges based on events built up over years (and, I assume, the preceding books).

The action, when it comes, is fast and furious; while there's not a blow-by-blow description of every punch or shot landing, in reality that's not the way things work, and I got a clear sense of the fight without the pace of the story being sacrificed to the description of it.

The political machinations of war receive their own focus too; and the observations around propaganda and the manipulation of opinion are on the nose in today's partisan political landscape – almost painfully so. To win a war, you need to maintain the support of your people, and although Aukes clearly wants us to root for the rebel forces against the Collective's leadership, she explores the opposing thought processes well enough that we understand why each side supports the actions they take, even though we might disagree.

Does dropping into the series partway through hurt this read? A one-page precis detailing a little Collective history might have been a useful addition to the book (matching the very helpful description of the planets of the Collective's planets in the appendix), but Aukes masterfully drops hints through the text that with a little thought let you form a picture of what must have gone on before. Readers picking up this book without having read the previous ones need not fear having "missed out".

Did I enjoy this story? Yes,

MA'AM! Am I intent on reading the rest of the series? <clickity click> Yes, MA'AM! Would I watch a Netflix series based on this story? Yes, MA'AM!

So, Edwin, what is *Fringe War* good for? It's *not* absolutely nuthin', I'm sure of that.

## Den Danske Borgerkrig 2018-24 (The Danish Civil War 2018-24)

**Author: Kaspar Colling Nielsen**
**Norwegian translation: Kyrre Andreassen**
**Cappelen Damm AS, Oslo 2018 (originally published in 2014 in Denmark by Gyldendal)**
**222 pages**
**Review by Megan Turney**

*Den Danske Borgerkrig 2018-24* (The Danish Civil War 2018-24) is an exceptional example of modern Scandinavian science fiction. Before delving into this absurd, wickedly satiric novel, I should preface this review with a disclaimer: I am very passionate about Scandinavian science fiction. In fact, I even wrote my dissertation on it. So, it may be a good idea to bear that in mind as I rave about my appreciation for this novel.

Part of my enthusiasm for this book can be traced back to the state of Scandinavian science fiction as a whole; although Norway, Sweden and Denmark have consistently published brilliant contributions to the genre, they are so rarely translated, and thus don't always get the international recognition that their English language counterparts tend to automatically receive by just being accessible.

So, to find such a unique and absorbing science fiction novel actually set in Denmark, revolving around Danish society and written in Danish (but translated into a few other languages already), my interest was piqued and my expectations were high. Unfortunately, it has yet to be translated into English, so although I have high hopes that it will be accessible to even more English language readers in the near future, this review is, for now, mainly for any fans of Scandinavian science fiction, or for anyone interested in reading more about those obscure, foreign language contributions to the genre.

I had actually read a few samples of *Den Danske Borgerkrig 2018-24* in Danish last year, but was pleasantly surprised to find the Norwegian translation for sale in my local Tanum book shop in Norway a few months ago. I thoroughly enjoyed Kaspar Colling Nielsen's writing style in the original, and the Norwegian translator, Kyrre Andreassen, has truly captured Colling Nielsen's shocking, darkly comical and heavily satiric narrative voice. From what I've read in other people's reviews of the novel, this style is not for everyone; indeed, there really was no topic off limit and no expletive too vulgar. Yet, what with neither Norwegian nor Danish being my mother tongue, I wouldn't blame any native Scandinavians for wholeheartedly disagreeing with me in this review! However, I personally found this bizarre, unapologetically blunt novel refreshing; in such a boundary-pushing genre as science fiction, it was great to find an author that could not only conceive such a captivating story, but deliver it in an equally thought-provoking and entertaining manner.

The title of this novel is rather deceptive though; although it does revolve around the fictional Danish Civil War of 2018-24, the novel is actually set several hundred years in the future, with the protagonist, a 475-year-old Danish man (accompanied by his 350-year-old talking dog, Geoff), telling the reader about the circumstances and events building up to the war, and the subsequent state of affairs in the centuries thereafter. The key aspect that makes this science fiction is, of course, the fact that the narrator is an inhumanly old man, having been born into a hippy collective, inherited his parents' entire fortune as a young man and, following the war, had taken part in a developing stem-cell programme that essentially gave him the gift of immortality... and a talking dog. As aforementioned, a significantly exciting element of this novel is that it is authentically Danish; although the protagonist does discuss how the global financial collapse that contributed to the outbreak of a civil war in Denmark affected other countries throughout the Nordic region, Europe, and further afield as well, it was fascinating to read and explore the potential Danish reactions to what seemed like universal and troublingly foreseeable triggers of war. This was especially so seeing as the civil war raged between the majority of the population and the wealthiest tiers of society; an interesting concept in a country often considered to have one of the happiest societies in the world, a successful welfare state, and for having been responsible for the international obsession with *hygge*.

Colling Nielsen strikes the right balance between detailed explanations of events leading up to and during the war, and highly surreal yet surprisingly moving intermittent short stories that delve into snapshots of society before, during and after the war from all sorts of perspectives. In fact, these short stories that the protagonist has picked up over the centuries and relays to the reader seem fairly inconsequential to the novel as a whole, but by the concluding chapters of post-war life in Denmark, it becomes clear how subtly they all relate to the universal effects that war has on any society. I doubt that the book would be as gripping as it is, had Colling

Nielsen did not inject these vivid and poignant depictions of humanity against the backdrop of a political conflict that seems worryingly probable in the current political and economic climate.

These stories only become more absurd, grotesque and farcical throughout the novel as well; I think it's best that I don't list too many examples of these as I definitely found that the shock-value in some of the more tragic and disturbing stories added to the overall reading experience. However, to just touch upon some examples of my favourite stories, they included: a retelling of a story told by another talking dog (not Geoff, but a friend of Geoff's) that was very reminiscent of *Isle of Dogs*; a hilariously dark analogy of Winnie the Pooh; and a story that serves as a testament to Nielsen's impeccable writing skills by somehow making me empathise with a tomato.

As is probably abundantly clear by now, I would thoroughly recommend *Den Danske Borgerkrig 2018-24* to fans of Scandinavian science fiction. I can easily say that this has been one of the best Scandinavian science fiction novels that I've read and could genuinely consider it to be one of my new favourite science fiction books in general. I would be very surprised and disappointed if this doesn't get translated into English in the next few years. If it does, it is certainly one to consider reading, not just as a great example of Scandinavian science fiction, but as an unnervingly satirical, morbid and engaging contribution to the genre as a whole.

## The Last Tsar's Dragons
**Jane Yolen and and Adam Stemple**
**192 pages**
**Tachyon Publications**
**Reviewed by Eris Young**

*The Last Tsar's Dragons* is a fantastical reimagination of the last days of the Romanov dynasty and the first days of communist rule in Russia. Written by the powerhouse duo of fantasy Jane Yolen and her son, Adam Stemple, a prolific novelist in his own right, and clocking in at only 182 pages, the book is a whirlwind tour through one of western history's most hallowed eras. The story follows a handful of characters – a tsar, a tsarina, and a mixed cast of advisors and rebels – through complex machinations, brutal violence, grief, anxiety and jealousy. And of course to complicate matters there are also dragons!

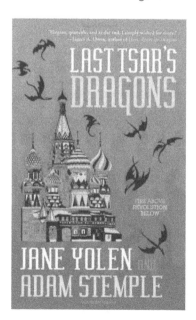

A story of this size must by necessity be fast-paced, quickly immersing the reader and avoiding deluging them with information, a constant danger in historical novels – and in other hands this story might indeed have become clumsy or cumbersome. But Yolen and Stemple manage it with aplomb, and while they might not have enough time or space to dig too deeply into every aspect of the complex dynamics at play during the fall of the Russian monarchy, they nonetheless manage to handle real historical figures and challenging themes deftly – often with dark humour.

In fact, the book likely benefits from the shared point of reference with most western readers: even if we've not seen *Anastasia*, we've probably at least heard of the Romanovs, Rasputin, and the Bolsheviks. In this way the authors are able to avoid having to say too much before getting into the meat of the story, and the fertile soil of an era rich in theme.

Using the space they have, Yolen and Stemple quickly get down to the business of interrogating class struggle, minority oppression, revolutionary violence and anti-Semitism. *The Last Tsar's Dragons* features a cast of characters who are almost all real people – from Rasputin and the Romanovs to the unexpected appearance of some famous communists – and to a one they are all unlikeable, in their own unique way. But where in another rendition this might have been off-putting, the strong voice of each character instead comes off as historically believable, and all the more engaging for it.

Yolen and Stemple glorify nothing. There is no hint of the romantic varnish that popular media so often tries to paint this era with. For Yolen and Stemple, dictators are dictators, anti-Semites are anti-Semites, and neither the Romanovs nor the Bolsheviks are heroes – if anything the heroes are the dragons!

Overall *The Last Tsar's Dragons* is cheeky, wry, gruesome and sometimes shockingly dirty. It glorifies no one, poking fun at the characters in a style that reminded me a bit of Bulgakov. The authors are clearly masters of their form, with a well-proportioned story that doesn't necessarily get too in-depth into character or historical detail. But the book is not meant to be a character study, or a completely new alternate history. It is speculation, not only because of the inclusion of the dragons but also speculation about the mindset of the characters – real people – in the final days of a very long epoch, and as such it performs admirably.

## The Forgotten Girl
**Rio Youers**
**352 pages**
**Titan Books**
**Review by Samantha Dolan**

It's been a lean summer for me so far when it comes to reading material. While I was waiting for the fifth Pierce Brown book to be released, I was hoping to find something that would light a literary fire under me. And then I started *The Forgotten Girl*.

This novel is unapologetic in its pace and violent detail. In the first few pages, you think you've stumbled into a gangster novel as you plunge headlong into a vicious beat-down. Then you meet the Spider and you, like our unlucky protagonist Harvey, have no idea what's happening but you're along for the duration whether you like it or not.

Harvey is a busker, making a living on the streets of New Jersey. He's described as a white guy with dreadlocks, following a routine that keeps him ticking along nicely. While he's at great pains to make sure the reader knows he's not a coward, he also doesn't come across as someone who is massively ambitious. He seems to be happy to be defined by all the things he's not and is a passive but not unpleasant leading man. The most fascinating thing about Harvey, in my opinion, is that biggest thing that he is not; part of the main story. I know, that sounds like an oxymoron when discussing the protagonist but he really is on the periphery of a situation that started decades earlier. And as Harvey worms his way deeper into a narrative that isn't his own, the reader starts to get an idea of the scope of this new world. It's quite impressive.

*The Forgotten Girl* is about a girl Harvey knows as Sally. She's being hunted by The Spider because she's taken something from him that's left him greatly diminished and he wants it back. Sally has been on the run for years and able to evade The Spider until she fell in love with a busker from New Jersey. Through Harvey's eyes, we learn how Sally met The Spider and how she became his titular forgotten girl.

Youers' world is rich and deep

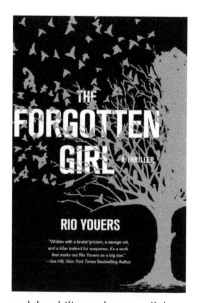

and the ability to draw parallels between his world and the one we all share is easy and disturbing. The character development is slow but purposeful and while the goons are pretty much interchangeable, Harvey's relationship with his father is a highlight. It is also immensely satisfying to see Harvey grow and change and start taking positive action instead of allowing life to happen to him constantly. But this was one of those books that you just wanted to race through to know what happened and slow right down so you can savour every twist and turn. This was definitely going to be my first 5-star review of the year but about two-thirds of the way through, we hit a pothole that almost took the wheels off.

"When my boss has finished with the girl, she's ours ... And let me tell you, Harvey, we're not interested in her mind."

It is made clear that these are

bad guys. It is made abundantly clear how many ways they can hurt you. The level of creativity in this whole novel is top notch so why resort to sexual violence against women? Being a rapist shouldn't be a character trait. And frustratingly, it's not the only time this comes up. It just does nothing to advance the story or the characters' development and it feels like just a 'thing' that happens because that's what happens to women in bad situations. It really brought me out of the world and I never really got back into it.

It's a massive shame because the ending is satisfying and everything up to that point feels authentic and exciting. I think that the proliferation of sexual violence against women in entertainment should be curbed. We should just come up with better ideas. But that being said, the ideas in Rio Youers' book are first class: it was a fast and fabulous read.

## The Migration
**Helen Marshall**
**Titan Books £8.99**
**Review by Ian Hunter**

Billed as being creepy and atmospheric, and evocative of Stephen King's classic *Pet Sematary*, *The Migration* is a story of sisterhood, transformation, and the limitations of love, from a thrilling new voice in Canadian fiction.

"When I was younger I didn't know a thing about death. I thought it meant stillness, a body gone limp. A marionette with its strings cut. Death was like a long vacation a going away."

Storms and flooding are worsening around the world, and a mysterious immune disorder has begun to afflict the young. Sophie Perella is about to begin her senior year of high school in Toronto when her little sister, Kira, is diagnosed. Their parents' marriage falters under the strain, and Sophie's mother takes the girls to Oxford, England, to live with their Aunt Irene. An Oxford University professor and historical epidemiologist obsessed with relics of the Black Death, Irene works with a centre that specializes in treating people with the illness. She is a friend to Sophie, and offers a window into a strange and ancient history of human plague and recovery. Sophie just wants to understand what is happening now; but as mortality rates climb, and reports emerge of bodily tremors in the deceased, it becomes clear there is nothing normal about this condition and that the dead aren't staying dead.

When Kira succumbs, Sophie faces an unimaginable choice: let go of the sister she knows, or take action to embrace something terrifying and new.

Tender and chilling, unsettling and hopeful, *The Migration* is a story of a young woman's dawning awareness of mortality and the power of the human heart to thrive in cataclysmic circumstances.

Let's get that *Pet Sematary* comparison out of the way first. This is no *Pet Sematary*, and it's not meant to be, so readers will be disappointed if that's why they bought *The Migration*. *Pet Sematary* was an out-and-out horror novel, and one of King's best where he tackled something truly horrific to his mind – the death of his children, and what lengths he would go too if he could do something about it. This is something far more subtle, and creepy, and dare I say, better written. Marshall's prose is lyrical, poetic, and dream-like, conveying perfectly the sense of confusion in Sophie's mind and those around her as they react to two world-changing events.

Marshall also has some advantages over King in her ability to write a believable young heroine. Not that King can't, but no matter how good a writer he is, Marshall has the advantage of having been a young woman, and can draw on her experiences of living in Canada and moving to England, as Sophie is forced to do. Marshall is also an expert in the Black Death, having a PhD in Medieval Studies and a postgraduate Fellowship from Oxford University where she investigated literature written during the time of the Black Death – handy knowledge to have.

As I write this review, Europe has just sweated through a heatwave, and perhaps one of many to come due to global warming, but it was clear that the transport infrastructure for rail and air travel couldn't cope with extreme temperatures. Meanwhile in Australia, birds have been found to carry antibiotic-resistant superbugs which potentially could leap between species, and possibly to humans. Is a scenario where climate and disease combine to change the world forever that far-fetched? Who knows, but *The Migration* is one of those crossover novels of recent times – think of Claire North, whose books straddle the worlds of literature and speculative writing to appeal to a wider audience and be nominated for major speculative fiction awards at the same time (Clarke, BSFA, Campbell, and winning a World Fantasy Award). This is more than Young Adult, more than zombie apocalypse, more than horror, even though aspects are horrific and downright creepy, and while I can't predict the future, I'm pretty confident *The Migration* will be appearing on the shortlists for awards in 2020.

## The Plague Stones
James Brogden
Titan Books, 419 pages
Review by Benjamin Thomas

James Brogden's *The Plague Stones* is a gothic world of horror and history. The novel follows a London family: mother, father, and son, as they leave the city following a violent break-in and become the inheritors of an isolated property in Holiwell village. As the family becomes accustomed to the odd ceremonies regarding plague stones that they find scattered around, things begin to take odd turns. Visions of a dead girl plague the family, and underlying tensions begin to bubble to the surface, leaving the reader with no other choice but to frantically turn the page and find out if they will survive the horrors of Holiwell, and of those of their own, more personal making.

Brogden's writing drew me in from the very beginning of the novel. He has a knack for horror, and a skill on judging just how much should be revealed and at what times. As the family begins to descend into madness, Brogden continues to let little bits of history escape, carefully avoiding information dumps, as well as long, drawn-out passages that could potentially bore readers. The novel's pacing is pristine and never lets up. He is creative in the way he passes information to the reader: using a school history teacher and a question asked in class, as well as dialogue.

Part of the narrative takes place in the 1300s, and at no point did I feel Brogden's depiction of that time or the true horrors of the plague were misrepresented in anyway. His writing has a unique quality: you believe it wholeheartedly. Not only is the suspension of disbelief present and accounted for, the novel's pacing and tension

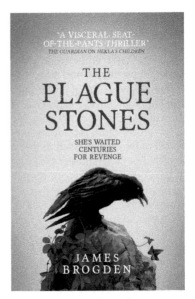

'A VISCERAL SEAT-OF-THE-PANTS THRILLER'
*THE GUARDIAN ON HEKLA'S CHILDREN*

THE
PLAGUE
STONES

SHE'S WAITED
CENTURIES
FOR REVENGE

JAMES
BROGDEN

remain steadfast throughout.

A singular qualm with *The Plague Stones* is the numerous backstories. Each member of the family has their own issues, and while these being present can lead to deepening feelings toward a character, they were slightly distracting in this novel. I want to point out that I think each one was developed and engaging, but I wanted more of the main story, and while I didn't get annoyed or bothered by the side plots, I definitely wanted to turn the pages slightly faster while reading those sections, if only to get back to the main, vengeful, story line.

*The Plague Stones* landed in my lap while I was on the look for a good horror novel. It did not disappoint. James Brogden wove together a tense, macabre novel that would be a perfect read for the coming fall.

## The History of Science Fiction (Second Edition)
Adam Roberts
Palgrave Macmillan
548 pages
Review by Teika Marija Smits

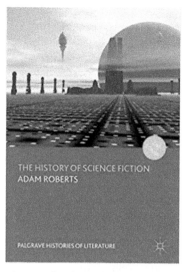

Approaching a subject as tricksy as science fiction, Roberts, quite rightly, begins his history with definitions. In essence, he reviews various critics' attempts to describe what science fiction is, but then points out that those definitions are widely debated.

"The present study has been unable to avoid the, often, tedious debates concerning definition, but my aim is to present a historically determined narrative of the genre's evolution rather than offering an apothegmatic version of the sentence 'SF is such-and-such'."

Roberts certainly succeeds in his aim. He covers a lot of history – first examining the potentially science fictional texts of some 2,000 years ago (i.e. the novels of the classical era), and then proceeds chronologically. Predictably, less than 200 pages are given over to the centuries preceding the 20th century, and a further 300 pages given to the science fiction of the 20th and 21st centuries. Yet for all Roberts' apparent caution in providing a definitive explanation of what exactly science fiction is, he is very clear that:

"Fantasy is supernatural, SF extraordinary, and there is the world of difference between those two terms. Once we accept that a wizard is a form of priest, we see that there is always a priest in fantasy. This priestly role is almost always taken (in effect)

by a technological artefact in SF."

Roberts' central thesis is that science fiction, as an easily recognizable genre of writing, fully emerged in the period of the Protestant Reformation in the 17th century when Copernicus's radical new worldview – that the Earth revolved around the Sun – really took hold in Europe, a key event of this time being the execution of Giordano Bruno the Nolan. Bruno was burnt at the stake by the Catholic Inquisition for his religious, philosophical and astronomical views. (Bruno held fast to the idea of cosmic plurality and an infinite universe.) Unlike Brian Aldiss (and many others) who propose that Mary Shelley's *Frankenstein* is the true starting point of science fiction, Roberts believes that Kepler's Somnium, written in the decade after Bruno's martyrdom for science in 1600, is 'the first unambiguously science fiction novel'.

It is difficult to argue with Roberts' reasoning, yet, it will be contested because the science of the 17th and 18th centuries (as well as the classical era) bears so little resemblance to science – and technology – as we know it today. However, whether you fully agree with Roberts' thesis, or not, doesn't really matter since the book succeeds in its main aim to deliver 'a historically determined narrative of the genre's evolution'. Highly inclusive, indeed comprehensive, it covers the works of hundreds of science fiction writers, expanding greatly on those novels by some of the most significant and well-known contributors to the field. (There is a whole chapter on the works of Verne and Wells.) Significantly, Roberts also covers the evolution of science fiction on the big and small screen, concluding that SF in prose form is only a small – and relatively insignificant – part of the science fiction universe nowadays, when you consider the impact of *Star Wars* and the way science fiction, as visual extravaganza, is now part of mainstream culture.

Though largely academic in nature, Roberts' writing is engaging, his observations thought-provoking and occasionally humorous, his close readings of many famous texts enlightening. I particularly appreciated Roberts' insightful remarks on the 'ghetto-isation' of science fiction, i.e. the way it is boxed into a clearly delineated literary genre, and the subsequent negative effects this has had for writers and literature in general.

Roberts' approach is analytical and all-encompassing. He draws from a wide range of esoteric sources, and develops his ideas with critical deftness. Even when his arguments seem provocative or idiosyncratic, they demonstrate an astonishing breadth and depth to his research. Roberts' evaluations of some of the writers and their novels won't be to every science fiction fan's liking – there's an impossible task! – however, Roberts' comprehensive tome *is* a necessary addition to every fan's bookshelves, covering the great texts, the not-so-greats and the plain overlooked in the wide, wonderful field that is science fiction.

CONER '17

## BECOME A PATRON

*SHORELINE OF INFINITY* HAS A *PATREON* PAGE AT

WWW.PATREON.COM/ SHORELINEOFINFINITY

ON *PATREON,* YOU CAN PLEDGE A MONTHLY PAYMENT FROM *AS LOW AS $1* IN EXCHANGE FOR A *COOL TITLE* AND A *REGULAR REWARD.*

ALL PATRONS GET AN *EARLY DIGITAL ISSUE* OF THE MAGAZINE QUARTERLY AND *EXCLUSIVE ACCESS* TO OUR PATREON MESSAGE FEED AND SOME GET *A LOT MORE.* HOW ABOUT THESE?

*POTENT PROTECTOR* SPONSORS A STORY EVERY YEAR WITH FULL CREDIT IN THE MAGAZINE WHILE AN *AWESOME AEGIS* SPONSORS AN ILLUSTRATION.

*TRUE BELIEVER* SPONSORS A *BEACHCOMBER COMIC* AND *MIGHTY MENTOR* SPONSORS A COVER PICTURE.

AND .... OUR HIGHEST HONOUR ... *SUPREME SENTINEL* SPONSORS A *WHOLE ISSUE* OF SHORELINE OF INFINITY.

ASK *YOUR FAVOURITE BOOK SHOP* TO GET YOU A COPY. WE ARE ON THE *TRADE DISTRIBUTION LISTS.*

'R BUY A COPY *DIRECTLY* ROM OUR *ONLINE SHOP* AT

WW.SHORELINEOFINFINITY.COM

OU CAN GET AN *ANNUAL* UBSCRIPTION THERE TOO.

KINDLE FANS CAN GET SHORELINE FROM THE *AMAZON KINDLE STORE*

## Captain Kirk visits the Oxgangs Mum and Baby Group

He doesn't have a baby. It's awkward.

He talks into an out-moded flip phone
which he holds in front of his mouth
the way people used to do when we thought
mobile phone signal gave you brain cancer.

A baby gargles. Kirk leans towards the mother.
"I think that's Klingon for
TODAY IS A GOOD DAY TO DIE,"
he says helpfully.

The mother must be a Vulcan. She seems unimpressed.

He can't cross his legs properly in the tight lycra uniform
and he doesn't know any of the words to 'Wind the Bobbin Up'
but he makes the tea without complaint
after that first day when he'd asked why
they didn't just get one of the yeomen to do it
and they made him write an apology letter to Janice Rand.

Sometimes the children cry, and there's nothing he can do to stop it.
Sometimes they won't eat, and the mothers let loose
the words 'failure to thrive' like a bank of phaser fire.
Kirk learns helplessness. He finds himself
waking at night in the red light of his Captain's quarters
as if there's someone crying for him.

He comes red-eyed to the group and his weariness is
mirrored in the women's faces:
worry lines, sagging gut, greying hair, inability
to cope.

They talk a lot about childbirth. More than one woman
is still bleeding. Kirk can't quite keep
the horrified expression from his face
and he's not sure if he wants to call Bones
or his mom, Winona, and tell her
he's sorry for every scar he's ever given her.

He tries to help out with the kids
but he's lightyears out of his depth.
On more than one occasion he contemplates the legality
of using a phaser set to a mild stun
on a toddler who won't sleep.

In the end he's asked to leave when one of the babies' first words is
KHAAAAAAAANNN!

He takes it well. More than anyone,
Kirk knows things are tough on life's frontiers,
where if you're going to go you might as well go boldly,
these places where no man.

*Rachel Plummer*


## Captain Kirk visits Edinburgh in August

He beams himself up
town to where it's busiest.
The people of this planet like to congregate
in places of religious significance,
such as bus stops, overpriced kebab shops,
or around a man dressed like Yoda.

He notes it all down in his log.

Visits a hydroponics facility
known as "The Meadows"
which grows students from seed
in some hidden glasshouse.
Upon maturity, the students
are each given a single disposable barbecue
and transplanted carefully outdoors
on the first warm days of summer.

It's lonely being an away-team of one
in a city so crowded.

Kirk registers for a poetry slam
under the name Tiberius,
though he can feel the old Directive
primed to take him out.
He recites some of the secret queer
love poetry he's been working on.
A lot of things rhyme with Spock.
He doesn't win
and one of the judges tells him
he needs to work on his poet-voice
which is "stilted" and "a bit too Shatner."

This planet doesn't deserve him.

He reminds himself that he could obliterate the entire city
with one well timed photon torpedo

and considers this option more seriously
after seeing his third political stand up show
and an experimental play about how smart phones are bad.

The people of this planet ebb and wane
like tides through nightful streets where light
is rockpooled under streetlamps
and each one of them is alien.

Kirk doesn't know how to phrase this for his report.

He goes back to the two-bed airbnb he's sharing with five other people
and thinks of his time at the Academy -
the dorms, the impossible tests, the performative nature of it all,
how for every ten of them trying to make it
only one would succeed.

He writes "Captain's Log, Stardate 2019. I've been. I've seen
the Fringe and all it has to show, the shows, the blows, the highs and lows
and this is what I've come to know:

Whatever you're looking for, it's not here. Three stars."

**Rachel Plummer**

---

Rachel Plummer is a poet, storyteller, keen knitter and former student of nuclear
astrophysics. She is a New Writers Award recipient and her latest book, *Wain*,
is a collection of poems retelling Scottish myths and folklore from an LGBT+
perspective.

# Bioelectric

Copying Tufts University worms
growing second heads
as we played bioelectric tunes
across dividing cells.
Our third-world laboratory
didn't ask where funding came from.
Next, frogs, some in bubbling spawn
others as tadpoles metamorphosed,
we learned techniques for extra limbs
prodigies that should never be.
With mammals one team reversed amputations,
joints coming at unexpected angles.
Another touched nervous system, brain
of embryos, stimulating certain lobes.
Locals following predetermined patterns
chose to arm themselves
with pitchforks, flaming torches
as they marched on us.

*Cardinal Cox*

# Jet-Ace, Retired

Just Logan now – stretching his pension
hoping nothing turns up needing cash.
Holo's on the wall of his years
in Royal Astro Force.
Cadet during Cassini crisis
politicians blustering over others' concerns.
Glad Britain kept out of Venusian war.
Tours on Ceres where they monitored
Jupiter and satellite states.
Triton conflict – craft stretched to limit.
Then first Martian campaigns,
Government always found someone
for men to fight on shortened budgets.
Now he's retired – robots pilot craft
over alien worlds – no regrets
no pity – just orders obeyed.

*Cardinal Cox*

---

**Cardinal Cox** is a poet and playwright, and was poet-in-residence for The Dracula Society (2015 - 2017). Out of this he was approached by a producer to create his one-man "spooken word" show *High Stakes* which has toured intermittently, including performances at Worldcon75 (in Helsinki) and Dublin2019 - an Irish Worldcon.

## Cataclysm Days: Andy Explains the Joys and Dangers of Hitching Rides

From the butte,
horizons lengthen.
Wrecked old world remnants—
melted metal
shattered cement—
become visible.
Mom knew its name.
It means less to me
than toys left behind
when we fled the fall.

Weird times changed humans.
Feathered folk roost here;
priests say otherwise
but I call them angels.
We pilgrims pray
for rides of grace
by the cliff edge
with outstretched thumbs
jutted toward a void
only wings could span.

Seraphim remain mute
after the ride ends.
Big wings mean small brains.
Predator status
endows flesh ripping
dentistry
unfit for talk.
Perfection in form
provides sufficient
reason for worship.

Angels select
lucky riders
for a flesh feast
pilgrims consider
an honor beyond
cannibalism.
Despite what chiefs say,
groundlings have always
feed divine hungers
before growing earthly corn.

The broken world below
earned apocalypse
due to natural
order rejection.
Greater beasts devour
lesser varieties.
Saying men can eat
bread made from undying
beings stands as heresy.
Gods eat mortals.

Half-chewed corpses
left by seraphim
halfway between
heaven and shattered sin
restore old balances.
I ache to bare
this throat to needle teeth.
Pick me sweet angel,
let this pilgrim ride.
let this flesh ascend.

**Chuck Von Nordheim**

# Cataclysm Days: Florida Switches From Melanin to Metal Intolerance

Even before the metal masters came, engine vibration stoked my libido.
Motor thrum and flywheel purr sounded out the susurrations of my desires.
I bent knee to NASCAR since the Palm Beach Baptist Temple neither hummed nor roared.

When fumes from a passing comet uplifted the Florida automotive fleet,
rousing sleeping chassis into sentient entities who jeered at flesh,
cosmic forces finally delivered deities I felt worthy of worship.

Some Floridians resisted granting civil rights to steel.
But those protoplasm bigots soon learned chrome always found the means to overcome,
whether through refusal-to-haul protests or exploding-gas-tank terrorism.

Our factory-built betters rewarded those who chose the right side.
We could transfer our minds to small horsepower frames.
I moved my ego into a Craftsman front-drive mower and never felt more fine.

My original body lounges in a convalescent home in Cape Coral.
Wrong-siders tend to my old flesh sack, though I've no plans to return.
What fool chooses an obsolete Edsel over a high performance stock car?

*Chuck Von Nordheim*

---

Chuck Von Nordheim lives in Dayton, Ohio, a location that provides much fodder for his poetical post-apocalyptic speculations. Currently, he works as a substitute teacher in Dayton area public and shares his life with his wife, Karen, who is smarter than him in every way.

You should never go into a cave,
Without taking along a slow knave,
When a goblin appears
With their knives and their spears,
You can abandon him off with a wave.
—*Lucy Finnighan*

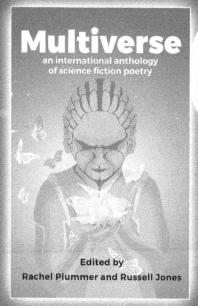

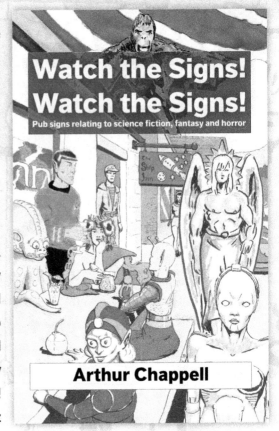

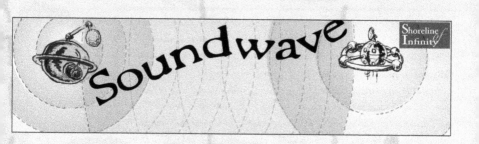

# New sci-fi podcast beams in from outer space

A new podcast from award-winning sci-fi magazine Shoreline of Infinity is launched, bringing the best fiction and news from around the galaxy.

Broadcasting from a satellite called Stella Conlator, Soundwave features audio dramas, interviews, music and poetry, all narrated and performed by brilliant voice actors.

"We believe in the thought provoking power of sci fi," explains host RJ Bayley. That's why we're inviting listeners to join our intergalactic Guild."

The first episode was released on the 1st of March 2019 and features Anne Charnock, JS Watts, Barry Charmon, Debbie Cannon, Sue Gyford and the music of Alex Storer.

Other great writers in series 1 include Richard A Clements, Catriona Butler & Rob Butler, and Matthew Castle, while The Infinitesimals will be creating and performing brilliant audiodramas.

Watch out for interviews with some stellar authors.

**Soundwave will be released twice every month on the 1st and 15th and is available in all the usual podcasting places.**

**for information and links to the podcast visit
www.shorelineofinfinity.com/soundwave**

From high in the hills the train was being watched. It snaked slowly across the open expanse of the former lake bed, its passengers completely oblivious to any danger. Everyone on board knew the enormous Dry Zone still supported an ancient indigenous population, the Mowok, but they all assumed none had ventured this far South for many many, years.

The old stories of Mowok raids, death and destruction were just that, tales from the past.

The expression, "Fear the Mowok", occasionally used by aged grandparents, was now something relegated to folklore, fireside tales, and threats dished out to unco-operative small children. What these travellers did not know was that, with its resources stretched to their limits, the Authorities were now struggling to contain the nomadic raiders within the depths of the Dry Zone.

Increasingly they looked enviously towards the farmland fringes. Soon the death and destruction will burst forth, a never-ending cycle, and the people along the edge of the dry zone will again learn to "Fear the Mowok".

This extract, and the cover art for this issue of Shoreline of Infinity, are taken from the (as yet unfinished) illustrated novella "Twin", by Stephen Pickering.

On an Earthlike planet, two outcast brothers undertake a journey of escape and self-discovery. "A tale of two worlds, two brothers, two choices and one journey."